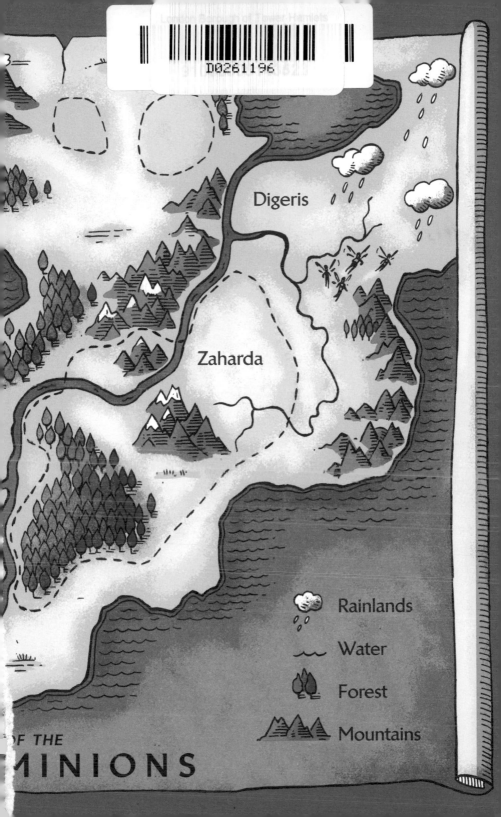

Digeris

Zaharda

Rainlands

Water

Forest

Mountains

OF THE

MINIONS

THE BOOK OF LEGENDS

What if all the stories were real?

Other books by Lenny Henry

The Boy With Wings

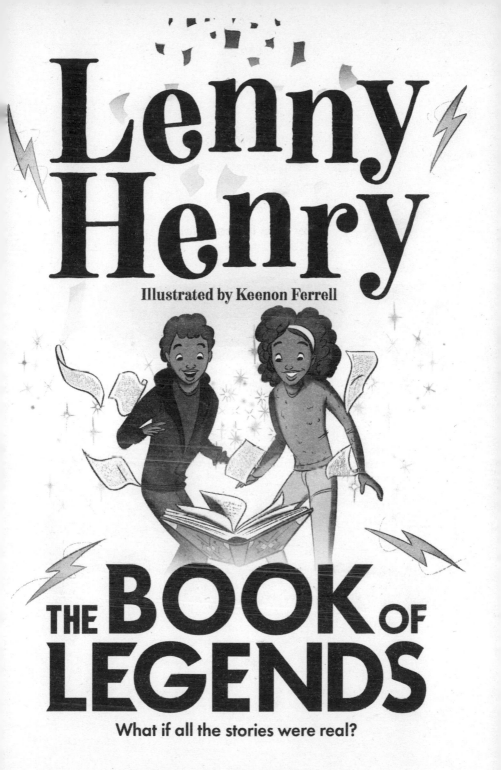

Lenny Henry

Illustrated by Keenon Ferrell

THE BOOK OF LEGENDS

What if all the stories were real?

MACMILLAN CHILDREN'S BOOKS

Published 2022 by Macmillan Children's Books
an imprint of Pan Macmillan
The Smithson, 6 Briset Street, London EC1M 5NR
EU representative: Macmillan Publishers Ireland Ltd, 1st Floor,
The Liffey Trust Centre, 117–126 Sheriff Street Upper
Dublin 1, D01 YC43
Associated companies throughout the world
www.panmacmillan.com

ISBN 978-1-5290-6786-6 Hardback
ISBN 978-1-0350-0467-6 Open Market

Text copyright © Lenny Henry 2022
Illustrations copyright © Keenon Ferrell 2022
Map illustration copyright © Fred van Deelen 2022

The right of Lenny Henry and Keenon Ferrell to be identified
as the author and illustrator of this work has been asserted by them
in accordance with the Copyright, Designs and Patents Act 1988.

1 3 5 7 9 8 6 4 2

A CIP catalogue record for this book is available from the British Library.

Printed and bound by CPI Group (UK) Ltd, Croydon CR0 4YY

To my Auntie Pearl and the staff,
past and present, at Dudley Library.
Thank you.

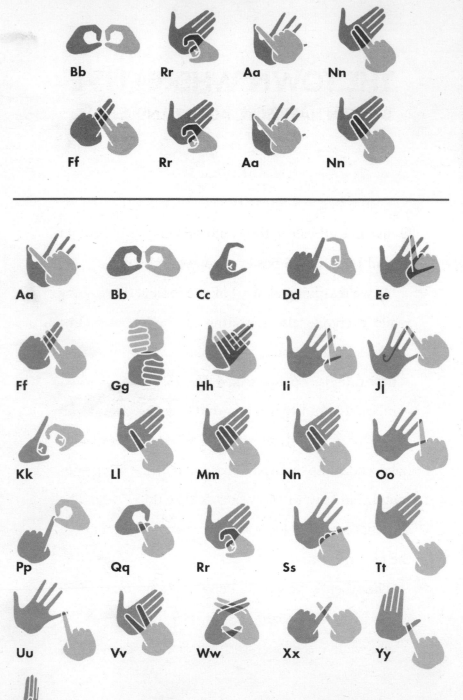

LEARN TO SIGN YOUR NAME

THE TOWN WHERE I LIVE
BY FRAN HARRISON, AGE 12 AND A HALF

I live in Ruthvale in the South Midlands. My brother
and I get the 76 bus every day to school.

As we're driving along, I like to look at the scenery
while everyone else is staring at their phones like
zombies. They should be looking out the window.
A new café has opened called Absolutely Kebabulous
– hilarious! And that playground by the garage has
finally been roped off – about time. So many kids
have ended up in A&E because of that merry-go-
round. No way in the world is that thing safe. The
slide has so many loose screws, it should be running
the government.

Then there's the woods. People are always surprised
we've got such amazing woods nearby – they think
where we live is all factories, motorways and chicken

shops. But Ruthvale's got more going for it than that —
although one of my dad's favourite jokes is:

'What's the best thing to come out of Ruthvale?

The A49 to Chester!'

My dad likes jokes like that. Sorry. *Liked.* He *used*
to like jokes like that.

He can be embarrassing sometimes. Sorry. He *used*
to be embarrassing sometimes.

Used to be that when we spoke about Dad we
didn't have to say 'used to be'.

Nowadays 'used to be' is normal for us, because
that's where Dad is nowadays. I hope wherever he is
now, he's with Mum.

Anyway, that's where I live in Ruthvale. I hope
that's enough for the project.

WHERE I LIVE

BY BRAN HARRISON, AGED 12 AND A HALF

Where I live, in Ruthvale, there's loads of people who look like me. Jamaicans, Barbadians, Saint Lucians, Guyanese people. It's a lot. You can get any type of food you want around here. The high street's like an all-you-can-eat buffet on a mad cruise ship.

I'm deaf. That means I go to a special school for deaf children though some hearing kids go there too, like my sister. She says 'it's like learning to be bilingual, and what's better than that?'

Leave it to Fran to find the 'fun' in learning.

It would be great if everyone knew how to sign, cos some of the pea-brains in our neighborhood take the mickey out of anybody that's different. I don't blame *them*, though. These things are learned, aren't they? If mum and dad are sitting there watching the news, moaning and complaining about 'foreigners', it's no wonder their kids say the same things.

People like a good moan in Ruthvale. One of the things people moan about is The Facility, which is this giant science-y place on the edge of town. I don't know what the problem is – they hire lots of locals. And it's not like they're doing alien autopsies in there. Although one time Fran and I went to snoop around and we did get a bit of a weird vibe from the place.

Ruthvale is a pretty boss town in my opinion.

The only part that's hard sometimes is having to work to be understood. I'd rather stay at home and make stories. My sister and I both love stories – and that's because of our mum. She loved storytelling. She read from books but sometimes she made up her own too. Those ones she wrote down in a big book for us.

My favourite types of stories are superheroes and adventures in weird places with heroes and villains and monsters and Vikings with enormous swords and dragons. Exciting stuff, the kind of stuff that doesn't happen in Ruthvale.

Sometimes, when I try to sleep, I'll imagine being in my own story. And then I'll wonder – when is my story going to happen? When do I get to be the hero?

But then two things happened to me – well, to us really. Me and Fran.

The first was four years ago, when my dad went missing on a camping trip. Actually, he was struck by lightning and his body was never found. I know! Dramatic.

Then, the second thing happened. I guess it was what our English teacher, Ms Rayford, would call a coincidence.

Let's just say that losing one parent to a lightning strike is unlucky. Losing two . . . well. It sounds like the beginning of a story.

CHAPTER  1

It had been a joyous camping trip.

All the way there, Bran, Fran and Mum were behaving like a family who hadn't lost a father four years ago. They were enjoying the drive to the campsite. Bran was making all the old jokes on the way there.

'Why is Cinderella bad at soccer? She's always running away from the ball!'

'What did the letter O say to the number 8? "Nice belt!"'

'I saw a snowman the other day. He said: "Is it me or, does it smell like carrots?"'

'What d'you call a little robot that's always going

the long way round? R2 Detour!'

(Mum and Fran usually joined in with the punchlines, even though some of them were so old they had whiskers . . .)

Fran and Mum sang along with that Whitney Houston song about always loving someone for ever and ever, which contained lots of high notes; Fran doing the main bit and Mum on backing vocals. Bran watched their expressions and signed things like,

'I'm so sorry I can't hear this. NOT!'

Then Fran pretend-punched him in the arm. He reacted in the usual way to that by signing 'Ow' repeatedly. Mum yelled at them both to calm down.

She had perfected one-handed signing while driving for important things, like 'STOP THAT!' and 'Who needs a loo break?' and, of course,

'We're nearly there!'

They set up the tents quickly and laid out their pyjamas. Mum's were pink and shiny and soft to the touch. Fran's were camouflage. Bran's were covered in dragon-riding, sword-wielding Vikings.

Once the tents were up and the bags were unpacked, Mum signed 'Pyjamas on, please. You've got ten minutes. We're going to drink a toast to Dad. I'm making hot chocolate and you don't want it to go cold.'

Soon, they'd thrown on their pyjamas, brushed their teeth, combed their hair and unzipped their sleeping bags. Nano-seconds later, Mum handed them a large mug each and they savoured the irresistible taste of hot chocolate, marshmallows and cream.

Mum took a sip, smiled then put her mug down and signed, 'To your lovely Dad. We will never forget you or your jokes, or the way you tried your hardest to fix everything. We miss you.'

She looked at the twins and smiled encouragingly. Fran went first. 'Dad, I was only eight when you left, but I do miss you and I wish you were here.'

Bran raised his mug, held it there for a moment, then put it down and signed, 'Dad, I miss you too. It's weird me being the only man in the family now.'

There was a pause as mum and Fran raised their eyebrows at each other.

'But,' Bran continued 'I'm trying my best to do what you would do. I know if you were here, you'd be telling us silly jokes and helping us to fix things. Like the time I came off my bike in the snow and smashed it to smithereens. It took a month to replace all the parts, but you fixed it in the end. If I didn't say so at the time, thank you. I miss you, Dad.'

And then he picked up his mug and took a gulp.

Mum looked at them proudly, and signed, 'You are the best, loveliest, most caring children anyone could ever wish for. I'm a very lucky mum. Your dad would be very proud of how you've turned out.'

She turned for a moment away like she didn't want them to see her crying. But it was too late for that.

'Do something,' Bran signed to his sister.

Fran glared at him. 'Like what exactly?' she signed back.

'What would Dad do? Tell the worst joke ever.'

Fran thought, and then signed, 'Mum. What did the ocean say to the beach?'

Mum wiped her eyes. 'What?'

'Nothing, it just waved.'

Mum smiled through her tears.

Fran loved her dad's jokes too, but remembering them always made her feel a bit sad. They were still funny but, even so, every joke was attached to Dad, and that hurt. Just then, another joke popped into her head:

"'Doctor, Doctor, there's an invisible man in the waiting room—"

"Tell him I can't see him now.'"

Bran laughed to himself, then burst into tears too. This grief stuff was hard.

Fran pushed up her sleeves and then signed: 'A snail got mugged in an alleyway by two slugs.

The police asked him if he could describe his attackers, and the snail said, "Not really, it all happened so fast.'"

They all laughed. And then they stopped laughing. Remembering the ridiculousness of Dad's jokes had made them all sadder somehow. It reminded them how much they missed Dad, so they stopped telling them and got into bed. Mum kissed them both on the forehead and told them to snuggle up in their sleeping bags and rest well. Then she asked them if they wanted a story, and even though they were both now twelve (practically grown-up), they said yes.

As far as they were concerned, their mum was the greatest storyteller on the planet. She told stories set in a magical kingdom where maidens get locked in towers and wizards battle lightning demons.

The big difference was, when she described the characters in these stories, the characters always *looked like them* (they were black or brown with thick curly hair usually in an Afro or hi-top fade or twisted into a braid); and even though the children liked other stories too – stories that featured lions, witches and wardrobes, or magical rings, or tiny people in fashionable bow ties and waistcoats – they preferred their mother's stories because the characters always resembled them, so it was easier to imagine themselves as the heroes.

And because Mum's stories were magical, or at least it felt like that as they listened, somehow the people and events featured in these tales would burst into life as Mum narrated and acted everything out. Mum began:

'This is a story about a girl called Yellowcloak who just wouldn't listen . . .'

The Story of Yellowcloak

There once was a girl called Yellowcloak, who lived on the tree-filled outskirts of a town called Koomoutya. She had jet-black hair, huge eyes and shiny brown skin. Before Yellowcloak's canny sorceress mother had died, she had hand-sewn the very cloak for which her daughter was nicknamed and enchanted it with charms, hexes and magical whatnot.

Koomoutya was a well-populated habitat for wild animals. Some of them were wilder than others.

For the last six months, their camp had been menaced by a mammoth and malevolent jackal called Jonjo. He was terrifying, and it was rumoured that he could pounce and guzzle you down in one gulp before you could scream, 'Oh my goodness, isn't that Jonjo?' He was that fast.

He also loved playing tricks on the young ones by

capturing them in the woods, spinning them round four hundred times, and then sending them home. Jonjo was a nasty piece of work.

One day, Yellowcloak got dressed. She combed her black curly hair and shaped it into two thick braids. She put on her walking boots and her gloves in case there were flowers or succulent fruits or juicy vegetables to pick. She told her Auntie Lisette that she was 'just going to see grandma and back in time for supper'.

Auntie Lisette told her to make sure she *did* get back for supper before dark, or there would be trouble, and she pulled on the end of her niece's plait just hard enough for her to go 'Ow'.

Mumbling under her breath about *people yanking on her plaits like they were at a tug of war or something*, Yellowcloak set off on her journey. Her lovely grandma lived several dead oak-tree lengths and then *left*, and then at least seventeen dead acacia-tree lengths and then *right*. That was how Yellowcloak remembered where she was going all the time: count trees and bushes and notice landmarks like rocks and dead trees – that should get you back home.

As she walked, a large lady with large muscles and a large Afro, wearing a leather jerkin and matching trousers, was chopping a tree into logs with an axe. She jutted her chin and said, 'All right, Yellowcloak? Don't stay out too late, y'know? Jonjo the Jackal is about and you're just the right size for his supper tonight.'

Yellowcloak sang her usual song, which was:

'La La La La La La Leee,
I'll do what I want, you can't tell me,
I'm quick on my feet and I've got my own rule,
You tell that jackal I'm nobody's fool.'

Can you believe that? She'd just ignored everything the lady said.

When she reached the end of the first batch of dead oak trees, she turned left, and she happened upon a kindly old man with long dreadlocks that reached almost

16

to the floor. His skin was the brownest of browns. His face had many wrinkles, but he was spry and fit for someone his age. He was picking herbs for his supper.

'All right, Yellowcloak? It's late, y'know? You should probably head back home because Jonjo the Jackal is out looking for somebody just like you that fits perfectly inside his tummy.'

But Yellowcloak just sang her song:

'La La La La La La La Low,
You can't tell me anything I don't know,
Jonjo the Jackal has no brains at all,
If I meet him out here, he will surely fall.
My feet are like lightning, my mind is quick,
And if I see that jackal, I'll give him a kick.'

And she continued on her way, ignoring the sweet old man.

It was now very dark, but the moon shone down and lit up the pathway ahead.

She was just outside Grandma's house when a shadow fell over the door. It was a large shadow. The biggest shadow you've ever seen. It looked like a dark shadowy mountain with its own claws and teeth. It was . . .

JONJO THE JACKAL!

Yellowcloak opened her mouth to scream, but nothing came out. She tried to run, but her feet wouldn't move. Jonjo reared up to his full height. He was gigantic and terrifying. He growled:

'Yellowcloak, your problem is you don't listen to
    what they say,
They told you I would eat you, but you still came
    my way.
Your Grandma was delicious and you'll make a fine
    dessert,
Now just stand where you are, Yellowcloak, I
    promise this won't hurt.'

And he leapt towards her, and Yellowcloak howled as much about her granny being eaten by this horrible jackal creature as with fear – HOWWWWWLLLLLL!

Jonjo swept past her, his claw ripping her cloak and leaving a long red line down her arm. Yellowcloak screamed again and managed to jump out of his way. Jonjo spun round and snarled, rubbing his tummy in anticipation of his Yellowcloak meal. The girl had just two seconds to wish that she had listened to everyone's advice and gone home before dark.

And then he leapt at her with a ROOOOOAAAR!

Yellowcloak screamed and closed her eyes.

AHHGHGHGHGHGHGHGHGHGHGH!

And then an enormous axe flew through the air.

WHOOSH!

Suddenly, right there in front of her, Jonjo lay with no head on his shoulders at all.

Yellowcloak turned around and saw the large axe-woman standing before her. 'I followed you. Everyone around here knows that Jonjo is trouble. Well, no more.'

Yellowcloak was now looking at the long nasty scratch on her arm where Jonjo had clawed at her. The cut was deep, but suddenly the old man with the dreadlocks and the thousand wrinkles was by her side examining her wound. 'When it started to get dark and I didn't see you coming back, I was worried.'

And as he gently chided her, he squashed together some herbs and made a gooey ointment for the wound and bandaged her arm. That night Auntie Lisette made a celebratory curried jackal and rice with yam, sweet potato and breadfruits.

The big surprise of the evening was that Grandma had *not* been devoured by the jackal. She had slipped out the back door as soon as she had seen his shadow fall across her windowpane and run into the hills until she was sure everything was safe. There were great cheers when she arrived back at the celebration. Grandma listened to what had happened to Yellowcloak, then she hugged her and said,

'You see, child, you have to listen. There are things out there that don't wish you well. Now, let's eat.'

Everyone ate their fill and talked about past conquests and other naughty children who disappeared because they wouldn't do as they were asked.

Yellowcloak vowed that she would always listen to, and do what she was told by her elders, and from that day forward, she did.

Well, most of the time.

The End

Mum told the story and acted out every part. Bran and Fran enjoyed it immensely. Afterwards, they talked about the story and what it meant in detail. Bran signed, 'So, hang on a minute, this story is about listening to grown-ups? But doing what you're told isn't always the best thing, is it?'

Fran signed impatiently, 'Of course you should do what you're told, you numpty. Otherwise one day you might get eaten by a flipping great jackal.'

Bran scowled. 'Grown-ups get things wrong sometimes, you know. Plus, there aren't any jackals round by us. This is the Midlands! Besides, the axe-lady and old man were strangers. She shouldn't have listened to either of them.'

Fran snorted. 'If she'd listened to them, she wouldn't have nearly got herself eaten.'

Mum laughed. 'You two could argue about this all night. But if you do, then no ice creams tomorrow! Now go to sleep, the pair of you!'

Although Fran and Bran were safely wrapped up warm in their tents, they were both thinking the same thing. That camping without Dad, no matter how much they all tried to pretend, was still pretty miserable.

That night, Bran drew in his sketchbook as usual until he couldn't keep his eyes open. He made up stories about a monster-hunting Viking called *Bjorn: The Monster-Hunting Viking* (he was only twelve and hadn't quite got the hang of catchy titles yet).

He was an inventive storyteller, but this sometimes got him into trouble at school. The excuses he used to get himself out of trouble were masterpieces. But Fran and Miss Didion, the maths tutor, had Bran's number from the off.

Usually the exchanges went something like this:

Bran would sign, 'I was in the boys' toilets and happened to be holding my homework which I had worked really, really hard on. I was sure I would get an A or maybe even an A-star, and when I went to flush the toilet, a miniature hurricane appeared at that very moment, swept the homework out of my hand, down the toilet and it got flushed away.'

Miss Didion would reply, 'Really?'

And Fran would sign, 'Maybe. Or maybe if Bran thought about it he would admit honestly that he just didn't do his homework because he was too busy drawing Vikings with swords, and fell asleep.'

Bran would reply, 'I think my story's better.'

CHAPTER

Meanwhile, in her tent, Fran's head was pounding. It was as though the top of her skull had been removed, and human-sized mice were bouncing rocks off her brain. BOING! WHEE! BOING! WHEE! She couldn't sleep, mainly because she couldn't stop thinking of Dad when he was struck by lightning. Her mind zoomed back four years to a camping trip just like this one. Bran was dozing, clutching his sketch pad and pencils as he lay in his sleeping bag next door. Fran was finding it difficult to bed down in the tent, so when she saw her mum and dad's shadows tiptoeing past, she couldn't help but follow. She snuck out of her tent and tried not to snap any twigs or step on sharp thorns that would make her yell 'Ow' and 'Yelp' and 'Whyyyyyyyyy?' because that might alert her parents to the fact that their eight-year-old child was sneaking around behind them.

As they reached the top of the mound, with a full-fat milky-white three-quarter moon shining down on them, Fran watched Mum and Dad as they hugged and pointed out stars to each other.

In less than a heartbeat a hook of lightning flashed across the sky and Dad was gone.

Fran put all these thoughts of *what happened four years ago* in a box in her head (she'd become good at doing that recently. If something bothered you, you could concentrate and pretend you were putting that problem in a box and storing it somewhere in your mind until you had a solution.)

She heard the familiar sound of Bran snoring in the tent next door. She put her book down next to her pillow. It was a book called *Can You Survive?* that Dad had given her when she was little, all about how to dress a wound or fix a broken finger or what leaves to boil to make a tea that would help your digestion. It also had self-defence diagrams.

Her dad had taught her and Bran self-defence from an early age. Mrs Gadfly, their infant-school teacher, had eventually called their mum and dad in to discuss 'Bran and Fran's aggressive interactions in the playground'.

Dad had made them go round and apologize to everybody that they had hit, and Mum had taken over an assembly and regaled the captive audience with the story of 'The Little Girl Who Lashed Out'. She made the entire school laugh and cry and think about how punching, kicking, biting and yelling are not the only ways to get what you want.

It's no surprise that Bran and Fran's mother could enchant an entire school with her storytelling skills. She was, after all, storyteller in residence at a bookshop in town called Once Upon A Wow. There, she sold books and told stories all day.

She worked with an older lady called Madge who used to be a model a hundred years ago. Madge wore black-and-red stripey jumpers, short skirts and pixie boots, and had a shock of grey punky, spiky hair. She liked red lipstick and loved the twins. She thought their mother was a genius. She'd tell anyone who would listen, 'Oh, darlings, your mother's the maraschino cherry on the sundae, the jam in the Victoria sponge, the best fish and chips I've ever had – and you can tell her I said that, darlings. I love her to bits!'

And then Madge would tell the story of how they met.

She had been working in the shop when a young lady walked in looking stately and gracious and beautiful. Madge had been enchanted the minute she heard her speak.

'My goodness, aren't you gorgeous? You should be on the telly! Better than any of those dopey weather people they've got on at the moment. You could bring the sun out just by talking, darling.'

Their mother had smiled her radiant smile and put out her hand. 'My name is Effiya,' she had said.

Madge shook it warmly. 'Madge. Can I interest

you in a book? Poetry, memoir, celebrity biography?'

Effiya had said, 'Well, what I really need is a job and a place to stay.'

Madge had hesitated. Business was slow and as much as she wanted to help the stranger out, she wasn't sure she could take anyone on right now.

'I'm an excellent storyteller,' their mother went on. 'I love books about magic and adventures and romance and engineering. I want to keep making up stories and I could literally sleep anywhere; under a bed, on top of a wardrobe, in a matchbox even.'

And she dazzled Madge with a smile.

Just as Madge was thinking that this lady sounded rather like she was out of a storybook herself, a harassed teacher from the local school entered the shop with fifteen rain-drenched children in her slipstream.

'Sorry, Madge!' the teacher called. 'We've just been caught in the wettest downpour since Noah's Ark and we need to stay inside a minute.'

A boy with a topknot raised his hand. 'Miss, can I go to the boys' toilets please, I'm bursting?'

Three more children raised their hands for the loos. 'I'm bursting too, miss!'

A boy with Afro puffs put his hand up too.

'Miss, are there any crisps?'

'Salt and vinegar flavour?'

'Roast chicken!'

'Cheese and onion!'

'Anything but prawn cocktail.'

Madge had just blinked at all the questions. But, smoothly and efficiently, Effiya sprang into action.

'How about a story? But first . . .'

She escorted the children who were bursting for a wee to the nearest loos.

She put the kettle on, poured out small glasses of squash for the children, and snaffled ginger snaps and digestives from a cupboard in the kitchen. She organized the children on the rug in the story corner with warm blankets.

And *then* she told them a story.

How To Eat
Your Fear

Far to the furthest reaches of the Nine Dominions lies Unsayth, the coldest place *anywhere*. There, snow foxes wear three extra layers of clothing, polar bears huddle around cooking fires for extra warmth when no one is looking, and the humans that live there have a saying: even the *cold* is cold.

Unsayth is a tough place to get around: the locals use long flat pieces of wood to which they strap their feet and glide over the snow. The children have a flat board which the more skilful can manipulate and swizz and whizz and fly in and around and up and down the hills with great aplomb.

The Snopar family lived in a small house made of blocks of ice. They slept under thick animal skins, and the children were made to go out at the break of day searching for sticks of dry wood in the nearby frozen forest.

The youngest Snopar was a girl called Ropar – her dad thought it might be funny to have a daughter called Ropar Snopar. (His parents had named him Jopar and he thought, 'I'm not going to be the only one in this house with a silly name. I'm going to spread it around.' So the other children were called Nopar, Copar, and Shopar. His wife Jill thought he was a bit of a goose.)

The day's great firewood hunt was on. The children, wrapped up warm and each holding an ice-cream sandwich in case they got hungry later, exploded from their ice house and sledded, skied and boarded off in separate directions, whooping and hollering as they disappeared into the forest.

But Ropar held back. She had her new board under her arm and she was wrapped up so much she looked spherical. She didn't want to go into the forest. She was scared.

As she stood there being scared, an enormous amount of snow came down in thick pillowy flakes and stuck to her until she was practically wearing a suit of snowy armour.

She started to get cold and figured if she walked at least she would be warm. So she set off, thinking, 'Try not to be scared. Try not to be scared. Try not to be scared,' and found that if she said it in a rhythm she could get a good pace going.

She entered the frozen forest and a snow bear reared up in her path! Ropar screamed and the bear, who was of a considerable size himself, turned and fled, yelling to anyone who could hear, 'OH NO! THE SCREAMING SNOWBALL IS COMING TO EAT ME! I'M RUNNING AWAY!'

Ropar had no idea what was going on, but her confidence grew just a little bit as she walked.

The snow continued to fall, Ropar journeyed deeper into the forest. She began to keep an eye out for fallen branches or twigs because she knew if she returned with nothing, she'd get no supper.

As she scanned around, she saw a shadowy figure running between the trees towards her. It was a white tiger! Ropar screamed again, and the white tiger yelled, 'OH NO! THE SCREAMING, POINTY-STICKED SNOWBALL HAS COME TO DEVOUR ME FROM TOP TO TOE. I'M RUNNING AWAY!'

He turned on his heels and beat a hasty retreat as fast as he could.

She couldn't believe it. She was the smallest in her family, but now bears and white tigers were scared of her. She had just a little bit more confidence now and was brave enough to strut off deeper into the forest to the broken bridge across the river. Normally at this point, her brothers, Copar, Nopar and Shopar, would climb up a nearby tree, attach their boards to their feet and jump off, slide up the ramp, gather crazy momentum and leap across the river to the other side. No way was Ropar brave enough to do something as dangerous as that.

This time, however, Ropar was not scared. She climbed to the top of the tree, jumped off, slid up the ramp, gathered crazy momentum and started the leap across the river to the other side . . .

But as she was doing so, her twigs fell and her snowy armour dropped off. She just looked like little Ropar flying into the air with her feet firmly attached to her board.

Just then, an ice dragon raised its head from the river, and Ropar, having already scared away a bear and a white tiger, roared, 'I'M GOING TO EAT YOU, NOW RUN AWAY,' and the ice dragon dived back underwater as quickly as it came up.

Copar, Nopar and Shopar watched from the other side as their little sister sailed confidently through the air and landed on the other side of the bridge. She slid up to them and said, 'So this is where the really dry wood is, yeah?' and went off to collect her share.

From that day forward, Copar, Nopar and Shopar told everyone they knew what they had seen. Because Ropar had been brave enough to take those first few steps, she had grown and grown in confidence.

Sometimes, kids, it's good to do things that frighten you – you might come out the other end a stronger person.

The End

Madge watched this new girl dazzle her audience with vim and vigour and gusto and biscuits.

Finally the rain pattered to a halt, and as the children filed out, they all thanked the new storyteller and asked when they could come back. Madge was happy to tell them that Miss Effiya would be there *every* day from now on because she was Once Upon A Wow's new storyteller in residence!

There also happened to have been someone else in the shop that day.

Madge had been putting off repairs to the shop because business had been so slow, but eventually she had given in and asked Mr Fix-It-with-a-Van to help.

'There's a creaky floorboard, a sagging ceiling, a wobbly door and a dripping tap. With a discount obviously, sweetie-pop? I mean, we're an independent bookshop with barely fifty pence to our names at the moment. Surely if I gave you some ginger snaps and made you the odd pot of tea, you might see your way to knocking some money off your fee, darling . . . ?'

Mr Fix-It, whose real name was Ken, had liked

Madge, and was a fan of warm tea and good books, so he agreed to give her a deal.

He'd worked hard to fix all the creaks and leaks and squeaks, and was there doing just that when Effiya had walked in. He had listened, rapt, to the tale of the brave snowball girl. She had not only captured the children's imagination, she had also captured Ken 'Mr Fix-It' Harrison's heart, and within a few months they were married.

The twins, Fran and Bran, had arrived quickly, and Ken and Effiya moved from their above-the-shop flat into a little house just down the road from the bookshop. They were very happy there. Ken had enjoyed fixing everything he could find, and Effiya took great pleasure regaling the twins with her stories.

And then, on an idyllic family camping trip four years ago, Ken had gone, and the three of them hadn't been the same since.

CHAPTER 3

Since Dad had disappeared, Mum's storytelling had gone up a notch. She was good at seeing what kind of tale they needed; a funny story to make them laugh, a sad one to make them feel it was OK not to laugh, or one with a helpful lesson. The stories helped sometimes, but not always. Like when kids at school made mean jokes and called their dad Kentucky Fried Harrison. Or when Bran lost his temper and started a fight and Fran had to explain to a teacher what had happened.

Fran was lying in her tent thinking all these thoughts, when she heard her mum's tent unzip. She lay there a moment, then stuck her head out.

Her mum was walking across the field towards the bathroom facilities, with a roll of loo paper in one hand and a book in the other.

Fran could never afterwards say why she decided to follow her mum that night, but something made her pull on her trainers and creep after her. She tiptoed from the tent to the path and onwards, gaining on her mum every step of the way. Every time Mum glanced around, Fran would duck behind a tree or hide in a bush or make herself really small. She was curling herself into a teeny, tiny ball when there was a sudden rumble of thunder and the rain began to batter down. Huge raindrops the size of suitcases smashed through leaves and branches and pummelled the ground. Within seconds Fran was drenched, soaked through to the skin.

KRAKA-THOOOM!

As Fran watched, an enormous bolt of lightning, strangely shaped like a hook, seemed to reach down and snatch her mother up! Mum screamed 'No!' at the top of her voice. The lightning fizzed, sparkled and crackled some more, and then was gone.

And so was Fran's mum.

Watching the whole thing, Fran would later explain, as the campsite people wrapped her in blankets and made her drink hot drinks, it was like one minute her mother was there and the next there was a Mum-shaped hole where she used to be.

Once she had signed to Bran exactly what had happened, there was no comforting him. It was just them now. There would be no more camping trips or stories or hugs. They were going to be alone and they would only have each other.

And that brings us pretty much up to the start of *this story*.

CHAPTER 4

A aaaaaaaaaaaaaaarrrrrrrrrrrrrrrrrrrrrrrrrrrrrrrrrrrrrrttttt gggggggggggggggghhhhhhhhhhhhhhhhhhhhh!

If you opened the top of Fran's head like a cooking pot, this was the sound that would come out. You wouldn't ever guess that if you met her, though, because Fran was always polite and sunny and good at smoothing things over. You wouldn't know how many things were bothering her.

One of them was their Auntie Madge.

Madge from Once Upon A Wow had stepped up when Mum had disappeared into a flash of lightning on the hillside and had become Bran and Fran's guardian.

It had been a few months now, and living with Madge was . . . interesting. Fran loved Madge. They both did. But the honest truth was that, as wonderful as Madge was as a friend and honorary auntie, she was a less-than-ideal guardian.

The decision was made that Madge would move into their house for the time being. 'Less disruption for you both, darlings,' Madge had said, rather sadly because she loved her own little flat. She had descended on them, bringing piles of paperback books, suitcases crammed with vintage clothes, and handfuls of red lipstick.

If they looked down in the dumps she would sweep in and say, 'Oh dear, let's rally together like bugs in a rug and we'll be fine, won't we? Now run along upstairs and play or whatever and I'll get pizzas for all of us from Bony Tony's Pizzaroni!'

And then Madge would blink tears out of her own eyes (she missed Mum too) and pull on her leather jacket and dart out of the door to get them yet another takeaway.

Takeaway for every meal might sound like the ideal for most kids, but Bran and Fran were getting bored of it. One day, Fran had tentatively suggested that Madge *cook* something.

Madge laughed uproariously. 'I burn water, darlings, so no point waiting for me to rustle you up anything. If I can't microwave or send out for it – you can forget it!'

The other problem on Fran's mind was that Bran was becoming more and more frustrated with the other kids' teasing about their missing parents. It wasn't that it didn't hurt Fran too but Bran responded to the taunts of his classmates by lashing out. It was getting him into trouble.

One thing that would calm Bran was to sit down and read their mother's stories, which were all written down in a book she called *The Tales of Koto Utama and the Nine Dominions*.

Her mother's stories were always set in a fantastical place called the Nine Dominions, full of dragons and elves and wizards, and each time she had finished a story they would discuss the scenarios her characters faced and the solutions they used to solve each problem.

'You meet a Mud Monster at the forbidden swamp,' she would sign. 'What do you do?'

'I don't know,' Fran would respond, eyes wide. 'What do we do?'

'Why don't you think about what the Mud Monster wants?' their mother would ask. Bran and Fran would look at each other. What did a Mud Monster want? More mud?

'What does anybody want, really?' their mother would hint.

The children would always sign back:

'Love!'

'A hug!'

'Ice cream!'

'Loads of money!'

There were other scenarios too, like what to do if you were about to be squished by an enormous boulder or skewered by an elfin sword or

squashed by a giant's thumb.

But now Mum was gone. Sometimes, after Madge had clumped upstairs to bed, where she would read books about weird old rock musicians, then put on a Maleficent eye mask and shortly after *that* snore for England, Fran and Bran would open *The Tales of Koto Utama and the Nine Dominions.*

The book reminded them of everything that their mother did and said. It smelt of her too. The sweet fragrance of her favourite violet perfume wafted in and around its ink-stained and wrinkly pages.

And Fran would think that, despite all the problems and the pressure that seemed to be building in her head, and the ways that Madge was a decent person if not an ideal guardian, at least she had her brother and at least they both had their mum's book. That was something.

CHAPTER

The first Fran knew about Bran's World War Six-level shenanigans with the head teacher at school was when she was summoned from netball practice by a grim-looking teacher called Ted Brisket.

'You'd better come and talk to your brother,' Mr Brisket said. 'He's been in another fight.'

Fran went to the head's office. As usual, she found Bran sitting on the bench outside, his tie askew, the sleeve of his blazer hanging off and a slowly purpling bruise to the side of his left eye.

The boy next to him had a nosebleed and sat with his head back and a sock to his nose because he couldn't find a tissue.

Fran sat down beside Bran. 'What's up?'

Bran signed back. 'Oh, I don't know, what do you think? Our mum and dad disappeared with a bolt of lightning and they're never coming back and it feels like everybody in my class – no, not just in my class, but the whole school – seems to think it's some kind of joke and I'm not having it any more.'

Fran tried to hug him, but he shrugged her off. Her fingers flew. 'You've got to calm down. Nobody is the enemy here.'

Bran replied just as fast. 'We're surrounded by enemies! Simon Houston said Mum and Dad had been lightly grilled the other day, "Hold the tomatoes and the mayonnaise." And what about Ranj Patel? Every time it's break, he mimes being struck by lightning for his mates and they all wet themselves. Well, the next time he does that, I'm going to shove him up a drainpipe.'

Fran signed, 'Not sure that'll happen! He's a big lad. You'd have to use a pound of lard on his head to even start!'

She mimicked squidging him up a drainpipe. Bran laughed grudgingly. Then the head teacher stuck his head out of his office.

'Bran, Fran,' he signed kindly 'your guardian is on her way.'

As if on cue, Madge thundered down the corridor towards the head teacher's office. Bran watched her approach and closed his eyes.

The twins had always admired Madge's exuberant dress sense, but it was one of those things that was delightful in an honourary auntie and got a bit wearing in a guardian. Today Madge was wearing a red-and-black stripey top with a black skirt, biker boots and a bright-red leather coat. She looked like a postbox with legs.

Madge dropped dramatically to her knees in front of Bran. 'Darling, what's the matter with you? Do you want to be exploded?'

Madge was getting better at signing but she still made mistakes.

'Madge, slow down,' Fran said. 'You mean *expelled*.'

Madge leaned closer to Bran and tried to sign more thoughtfully. 'You're always fighting, you're always in trouble. Oh, sweetie-pop. Your mum wouldn't want this, you know?'

Hurt, Bran looked right back into her eyes and signed, 'You're not very good at guardianing, you can't cook, you've got no stories and—'

'Bran!' Fran leapt up, her own fingers moving fast. 'Stop it. Stop it before you say something you'll regret.'

But Bran didn't stop. 'And you're not our mum!'

There was a horrible pause. Then the head's door opened and he leaned out. 'Bran and Fran, a quick word before your, ah, auntie takes you home?'

The children went inside and Madge sank down on the bench to collect her thoughts.

What she was thinking wasn't very guardian-like, but she felt that if she didn't act soon, the twins would be in a hateful situation where they didn't like her any more and they'd do something silly, like run away. As she sat there, sure as anything that the head teacher was in his office telling Bran that this really had to be the last time, that they couldn't keep giving him more chances, that it wasn't fair on the other children, she finally admitted to herself that she wasn't *really* guardian material.

No plant survived in Madge's house for long. A number of cats had simply moved into houses over the road rather than be left in her care, and her only dog hitch-hiked back to the rescue centre to get away from her. The words 'Madge' and 'looking after things' did not quite go together. Like custard and barracudas, or hippopotamuses and Formula 1, Madge and children was a disaster waiting to happen.

Madge loved the kids, but she had never in a million years imagined being responsible for them. She shook her head. Then she had an idea. She thought to herself:

Madge, darling, if you had lost your parents like these two darlings have, a pat on the back and an extra helping of pizza isn't enough to feel better. You'd need a change of scenery.

The head teacher poked his head out once more and asked her to come in. Madge got up, took a deep breath and followed him into his office.

CHAPTER

Aaaaaaaaaaaaaaaarrrrrrrrrrrrrrrrrrrrrrrrrrrrrrrrrrrrrr
gggggggggggggggghhhhhhhhhhhhhhhhhhhh!

If you'd lifted the top of Bran's head off like a cooking pot, that would have been the sound coming out. He was incredibly guilty and ashamed about his outburst at Madge. But it was also, horribly, true.

That night, Bran was lying in his bed thinking; his sketchbook lay open by his side. He had been thoroughly scolded by the headteacher, and then by Madge, who had been rather quiet and thoughtful that evening and had overcooked them some pasta with brown sauce instead of the usual pizza. Fran and Bran had gone to bed early.

He had drawn a warrior with dark skin and blazing eyes, wearing animal-themed armour and, rather oddly, carrying some library books under his arm. Suddenly, his shoulders slumped. He really missed his mum and dad.

He hadn't meant to be so mean to Madge, but he *really* missed his mum's cooking. She used to make (Dad's favourite) jollof rice and a spinach stew called *efo riro*. She did this barbecue thing with meat on skewers that was the most delicious thing he had ever tasted. He missed all of that. And, most of all, he missed her stories.

One of the stories his mother would tell was called 'Cloud Blessing', about a girl called Blessing who had a rain cloud over her head all the time. Blessing was kicked out of her village in Digeris, one of the rainiest regions in the Nine Dominions. The people didn't want more rain. But when she goes to Evawhe, one of the hottest places, and her rain cloud causes things to grow, she is deemed a hero.

Mum would say, 'What can seem hard to some

people can be a gift to others – but you might have to move around a bit to find out which is which.'

Bran so wanted them all to be a family again. He missed those days of sock puppets and sandwiches, of forgetful dragons and clever princesses with numerous tricks up their sleeves.

He sighed, and remembered the conversation he had had earlier with Fran before they went to bed.

'It just doesn't feel as though she's actually dead,' Bran had signed.

Fran had nodded. 'I know. It's more as though she's . . . ceased to exist on earth.'

Meanwhile, Fran lay in her bedroom . . . thinking.

As she had been getting ready for bed, Madge had come into her room and shut the door.

'Fran, darling,' she had said. 'I wanted to discuss something with you. Get you on side, so to speak, before I talk to your brother.'

'Talk to him about what?' said Fran suspiciously. She didn't like leaving Bran out of anything that concerned him. Grown-ups were always trying to do that.

'About the two of you having a bit of a change of scene. Just for a while. Or maybe for longer, if you like it! I think it could do you both – well, Bran really, but you too – a world of good.'

Fran's stomach had lurched uncomfortably. 'What do you mean? Are you sending us away?'

'No! Well, sort of. Fresh pastures, darling, somewhere where you'll be looked after with more than just chicken nuggets and fizzy pop. Now, there's a boarding school up north called St Cuthbert's. It's a diverse school. It has a languages department, one of which is BSL. Everybody signs there – isn't that wonderful? It's expensive, but your parents left a bit of money in a trust for you and I can sell the flat and live here until you're old enough to decide what you want to do. You'll still come back here for holidays of course!'

She looked at Fran, her eyes shining. 'I spoke to your head teacher, darling, and he thinks it's a marvellous idea.'

Madge thrust a pamphlet from the school into

Fran's hand. 'See? Doesn't it look incredible?' Madge put a hand on her shoulder as Fran studied the pamphlet. The front cover was of a kid in a wheelchair next to a Jamaican-looking kid in a very smart uniform, both of them pointing to a castle-like building behind them with a sign saying *St Cuthbert's Boarding School.*

'So you *are* sending us away,' said Fran.

'I suppose I am,' said Madge nervously. 'But in the nicest possible way.'

'I'll think about it, Madge,' said Fran, through gritted teeth. 'Maybe let *me* be the one to discuss it with Bran though, OK?'

CHAPTER 7

F ran went to Bran's room – as usual, he was awake and sketching.

'Come on,' she signed. 'There's something I need to tell you. Let's go to the den though, shall we?'

It was colourful in the den. On one wall Bran had been allowed to paint a mural of Vikings and dragons and monsters. The magical creatures seemed to watch over them as Fran told Bran everything that Madge had told her.

As Fran had expected, Bran was furious. 'I don't want to go to St Cuthbert's! This is our home!'

Fran was despondent. 'We've got to, I think. It's obvious that Madge isn't coping. I think she's trying to do this for us.'

Bran nodded. He felt guilty. He thought that if only he had behaved a bit better, then Madge might not be at the end of her tether and trying to send them away.

He flipped through the pamphlet from St Cuthbert's. There were black and brown faces just like theirs, language labs and lots of different types of communication, and it also said there was a dedicated person with whom you could discuss your feelings if ever you were missing home.

'It does look pretty cool,' Fran signed.

Bran shrugged. 'That's not the point, though. We need to stay here. This is where Mum and Dad are from, and if – when – they come back, if we're up north in the back of beyond at St Cuthbert's, they'll never find us.'

'But they're not here any more,' replied Fran miserably. 'So now it's just a house in a town called Ruthvale.'

Bran shook his head. 'No. We belong here

because *they* did. Because they chose this place. It is where *we* belong and I'm not going to leave here.'

Fran stared at the room around them and felt a ping in her heart. Her brother was right. This was their home and they shouldn't be made to leave if they didn't want to. Her face became sad and morose.

Then Bran nudged her.

' "Doctor, my brother thinks he's a dog. What should I do?"

"Well let's get him on the couch and I'll have a look at him."

"He's not allowed on the couch." '

Fran gave a small smile. Then she signed, 'What starts with a T, ends with a T and is full of T?

A teapot.'

Bran made a face. 'That one's so old it's got a Zimmer frame.'

Fran laughed.

'The thing is,' she started, 'I don't want to go to boarding school either. I've been thinking, remember that time we ran away because Mum made us eat cauliflower?'

Bran nodded.

'With cheese on, yeah. We went to the woods by the garage and Dad came down and grounded us for two months with no TV, and he told us off for frightening them like that, but Mum . . .'

'Yes,' signed Fran. 'Mum said there were worse places to go than the Kindly Woods – that, often, the most unlikely places are the way to what you seek.'

Fran was frowning. 'Bran,' she signed. 'What do you think she meant by that? Do you think—'

But before she could finish her thought, Mum's launched itself off the nearby shelf.

CHAPTER

The book took a lazy turn around the room, as if experiencing flight for the very first time. It soared from left to right and rocketed towards the ceiling. It banked to the left, did several barrel turns before flying up to the light bulbs, and then power diving towards the table and landing open.

The children ran over and had a look.

The book had opened at a story called 'Escaping via the Kindly Woods'.

'Whoa,' signed Bran. 'Did the book understand us? Is this some sort of signal?'

'Look at this, Bran!' Fran held out a Post-it note that had been stuck to the open page.

For my beloved Bran and Fran,
who will surely understand that this book
*   here is grand.*
Don't lose it, that's not the plan.
Read this again and then some more
and then you just might find the Me you're
*   looking for . . .*
Love, Mum.

Bran and Fran looked at each other.

'Mum wants us to use the book to escape,' Bran signed.

'Not just escape,' Fran replied. 'To find her.'

Escaping via the Kindly Woods

I'll sing you a travelling song if you will,
Please fetch me some ham and I'll eat my fill,
Procure me some pop and some crackers and cheese,
I'd like some crisps, could you bring them here please?

For Koto Utama shuttle jumps that aren't hooks
You'd best listen to me, the brightest of books.
You'll find what you're looking for, we'll have such
    hoots,
Please pack torches and blankets and shelter and boots!

Get trousers and jumpers and coats and wool hats,
Get trunks and T-shirts, get shovels and bats,
Bring seeds and soil, from your garden is best,
I want water from north, I need stones from the west.

Take it all to a wooded place, away from the road,
Away from the lights and from dogs and the toad,
Please place all these things in a circle, then dance
In the middle of it all, it's your only chance.

When the woods open up, you'll see a bright shining
    light
Like a small sparkling sun, through which crows will
    take flight,
Turn your back on Ruthvale, walk into the trees,
And soon you'll be gone, in grass up to your knees.

You'll stop for a drink from your bottle and then
You'll keep walking and walking and walking again,
And you'll keep moving on, to stop would be reckless,
There are things waiting here that would eat you for
    breakfast!

So whatever you do, however tired you feel,

Keep marching in time with nerves of pure steel,

And then suddenly light will envelop you whole

And you'll see that you've almost reached your goal.

And if you turn back you'll see eyes looking out,

You may even see claws and teeth in a pout,

of the creatures following you but staying clear,

Just checking to make sure you safely got here.

And now you've arrived, step out into the sun,

Because Fran and Bran – your journey has *begun*!

Fran and Bran blinked. 'But how do we—'

Whoosh! They found themselves changed into warm clothes appropriate for evening travel.

Whoosh! Their bags were whisked out of the wardrobe and rapidly packed with all manner of items, from avocados to zeps (large sandwiches made from a long crusty roll filled with meat and cheese). Small packets of seeds were tucked into their bags too, and two mini shovels with collapsible handles.

Whoosh! They were speeding out of the front door and through Ruthvale, swerving the guy who walked around at night with his shopping trolley and the tough kids who hung out by the bus stop.

Then, in a trice, they were in the woods, spreading around the seeds and stones, as the song directed them to do.

When the woods open up, you'll see a bright shining light
Like a small sparkling sun, through which crows will
    take flight,
Turn your back on Ruthvale, walk into the trees . . .

'Look,' nudged Fran. 'There it is.'

Sure enough, through the trees, there was a distant, shining light – which seemed to beckon them on.

As they pushed through the undergrowth, the light flickered – and within that flickering there were shapes and figures and shadows like nothing they had ever seen, moving to and fro alongside, in front and behind them.

They trekked and trekked and trekked some more until they came to a fork in the path and stopped. The ground had become boggy and slippery underfoot.

'Which way?' signed Bran.

'I can't believe we're lost already,' responded Fran. 'I'm not sure this was a good idea—'

Fran was just about to suggest they turn around, when out of the bog rose a five-metre-tall creature that seemed to be fashioned entirely from . . . mud.

Bran and Fran began walking slowly backwards and off the path, giving the creature a wide berth.

'Is that . . .' signed Bran.

'Yes,' replied Fran, hands shaking. 'It's a Mud Monster.'

As their eyes fastened on it, the mud creature sank and disappeared into the ground, and within the blink of an eye appeared next to them, and reared up to its full towering height. It stretched out its arms and roared exactly as you'd expect a Mud Monster to roar. It sounded like a cement mixer gargling gravel, and although Bran couldn't hear, he felt the vibration of this racket as if he were standing on a giant washing machine on a final-spin cycle.

Fran and Bran shook with fear.

'It's going to eat us,' signed Bran.

The Mud Monster stopped growling and pointed towards a gap in the trees in front of them, down the left fork.

Fran signed, 'I don't think it's going to eat us. It looks like it's showing us the way out. Remember – what did Mum say everyone always wants? To be treated with respect!'

'Everyone does treat Mud Monsters like giant doormats,' Bran agreed.

He signed his apologies and promised to walk around all Mud Monsters in future.

Then they ran in the direction the Mud Monster had pointed.

'I don't know about this,' she mumbled to herself. 'I'm not sure we're doing the right thing. Madge will be worried. This might be a big mistake, I don't want us to get into trouble . . .'

She was running so fast, and worrying so hard,

that instead of being relieved when they finally hit a clearing, she tripped over a fallen tree and dropped the book. It immediately seemed to sit upright and the pages riffled through to a story.

A Girl Who
Was Trouble

One night, deep in the land of Zafun, a dominion of twisted trees and bushes of every shade of green where things just seemed to grow whether they wanted to or not, an Elven girl who was Trouble saw a shining star fall from the sky. An honest-to-goodness falling star! She took her telescope and her bag of goodies and snuck out of the house and ran towards where the star had fallen. She was about a mile into her journey when she heard someone go 'OW!' She turned and saw her little brother Gavi, who was in his pyjamas and carrying a straw doll.

'Gavi! What are you doing?' yelled Trouble. 'You shouldn't be following me. I'll get you in trouble.'

Gavi replied, 'Oh come on, sis, every time I follow you we have a brilliant time and there's always a spectacular story to tell about where we went and what we did. Remember the horrifying horse? And the sabre-toothed crocodile?'

Trouble did remember these things and prayed nothing as dangerous happened on this day. She pleaded with Gavi to follow the path back to the house, but he stamped his foot and screamed and started to pull his hair out one by one until he was allowed to go with her. Six hairs in, she gave up.

Eventually they marched for another two miles towards the fallen star, and then, a little way back, she could have sworn she heard a noise. Well not so much a noise, but someone going 'OW! OW! OWAAAH!' She turned and ran back, and found her other brother, Nesta, wrapping a big banana leaf tenderly around his entire right hand.

He was furious. 'Trouble, why would you tiptoe past my bedroom door, and sneak out the back with not even a whisper that you're off to have a precarious adventure with rhino wolves and dragon dogs? I'm disgusted with you.'

Trouble furrowed her brow with concern. She sighed. 'You can come too.'

The three of them, Trouble, Gavi and Nesta, walked and walked and walked and walked and walked until they found what they were looking for. It was a large smoking boulder surrounded by fluorescent lights that were giving off noxious stinky fumes. Trouble looked concerned.

'I don't think this is a star,' she said.

Gavi was also concerned, 'Have you seen this footprint next to it?'

Nesta had a look. 'What has three large pointy toes like that?'

Trouble, Gavi and Nesta followed the three-toed pointy footprints deep into the forest. It was dangerous and dirty. Not only that, it was slippery and slidey.

As they journeyed, they talked about their dreams and what they wanted to do with their lives in the future. Gavi wanted to be a brave knight and rescue people from dragons and demons and weaselly ne'er-do-wells. Strangely, Nesta was focused on the idea of creating a refreshing non-alcoholic fruit drink with bubbles that would satisfy a grateful public and become very popular. Trouble, on the other hand, just liked the idea of causing trouble. She was of the opinion that trouble didn't always have to lead to death and destruction – in fact, causing trouble could lead to something good happening.

Meanwhile, the deeper and darker the forest grew, the more all three of their souls were filled with a creeping, wobbly, ice-cold fear. Nervous as all get-out, Trouble yelled loudly, 'Hello? Three-pointy-toed creature, are you out there?'

But no one replied.

And then they found out why. They saw the cooking smoke first. As they emerged into the woodland clearing, they saw a troop of soldiers tying a giant chicken-looking creature to a spit. Trouble walked right up to them and said angrily,

'There you are! I've been looking for you everywhere. Where have you been?'

The soldiers looked at her quizzically. Why was this girl yelling at them like this? Trouble ignored them and said, 'Your mum and dad are looking for you everywhere.'

She looked at the soldiers sadly. 'He's an only child and far from home. If I don't get him back to his parents, they'll be ever so upset.'

The soldiers snorted. One of them said, 'If I don't eat that drumstick of his, my tummy will be upset.'

And the rest of the soldiers laughed. They continued to add sticks and dry branches to the already blazing fire. Trouble ploughed on. 'You see, if you cook one of his kind – they're called the Luck Creatures, by the way – it causes bad luck to everyone within a fifty-mile radius to where the eating takes place. Everyone gets unlucky. Men, women, fairies, kings, princes, dwarves, elves, little tiny fish . . .'

Gavi joined in. 'Cows, sheep, sharks, sea monsters . . .'

Nesta couldn't help himself. 'And soft-drink makers, landscape gardeners, vampires, zombies . . .'

The chief soldier looked at them. 'You mean, if we roast and cook this giant chicken, all those people will be angry with us because we have made them fatally unlucky beyond all reckoning?'

Trouble, Gavi and Nesta nodded enthusiastically. With great gusto, the soldiers began setting the three-pointy-toed creature free, and the next thing they knew, our heroes and the gianormous chicken creature were all walking very quickly back in the direction they had come from. They were soon at the big smoking rock. The three-pointy-toed creature stopped and said, 'My name is actually Malcolm. You have done me a very good turn, so now I will do you one.'

Malcolm glowed like a small sun before dialling it down a little. No one likes a show-off. He gave Trouble, Gavi and Nesta each a small gold coin.

'These are for you to wear for the rest of your

days – you will find
things might go a
little easier for
you from now on.
'Gavi, you will
become a great adventurer,
and rescue members of the royal family
in distress and defeat dragons, but your highest
achievement will be that of storyteller, for once you
have had all these adventures, you'll write them down
in the comfort of your own home whilst drinking pints
of orange squash and munching on a large pie.

'Nesta, you will invent a fruity drink with bubbles.
It will become very popular indeed.'

Malcolm then paused, and had a good look at
Trouble.

'You, young lady, will be troublesome for the rest
of your life, always saying the wrong things at the
wrong time. You will fight for what you believe and
you will not back down until the job is done. You will

upset the wrong kind of people for the right kind of reasons. You will be a hero.'

He pressed a button on the side of the scarred rock and it transformed itself into an enormous global-shaped luminous spacecraft. An entrance opened with a gorgeous *zhhhssshhzzzhing* noise. Malcolm flipped up his palm to reveal a jangly set of keys, and said, 'Shall we go and make some trouble around the galaxy?'

And that's exactly what they did.

Once Gavi and Nesta had been deposited back at the house, Malcolm and Trouble whizzed off around the known (and even some of the unknown) galaxies, leading uprisings against evil wizards and kings and witches and demons, causing immense trouble for those people wherever they went. Trouble spent the next few years of her life with Malcolm, fighting for the underdogs by being as troublesome as she could, until she met a kindly wizard, settled down and had a baby. She never regretted her choices. Malcolm, on the other hand, had never met a more troublesome person in his entire life.

The moral of the story, children, is that fighting for what you believe is never a *bad* thing.

Also, having a magical creature on your quest is always a *good* thing.

The End

As Fran finished the story, she became aware that she had been sitting reading for quite some time and that she couldn't see Bran any more. But then suddenly she could. Bran was sprinting towards her and looked terrified.

Fran leapt to her feet. Behind Bran was a black-and-white spotty horse-like creature with a long and sharpened horn growing from its forehead. They were being chased by a small swarm of what looked like bees, but were much, MUCH, MUUUUUUUUUUUUUUCH bigger.

Fran reached into her rucksack without even thinking. She pulled out the two mini shovels with collapsible handles. She threw one at Bran and signed,

'Help me get rid of these ginormous bees!'

And she began swinging her mini shovel in all directions. Bran followed suit and swung his shovel with all his might. They hit many of these

little things with a satisfying *thwack* and *pang* and *twung*, and the best one of all, TH-DUD-DUD-DA-DOIIIIIIINNNNNNNGGGG! Soon, the swarm retreated and buzzed loudly off into the distance.

As they flew away, Fran managed to get a look at a couple of them. Despite their gossamer wings, they were definitely not bees. They were, in fact, very tiny human-like creatures that were dressed in immaculate military-style uniforms that would have been cute had they not been so very, very angry.

Fran turned on her brother. 'See? This is just like Mum's stories. When you travel to places like this it's nothing but trouble. We need to run back to the woods and do the rhyme and everything and just try to get back home. I'm scared. I wanna go home.'

Bran signed back, 'That is not what mum's stories say AT ALL. They say adventures are good and they help you figure out where you're going in life and –'

At this point they were interrupted by the black-and-white horse-type creature, who trotted over to them as though he hadn't just been attacked by a vicious swarm of tiny-winged individuals.

'Thank you so much,' it said. 'I've never seen anybody whack a Murder Fairy like that before. You were kicking some seeeeeerious bee-hind. There's not many people in the Nine Dominions who can say that.'

Still slightly shocked, Fran turned to Bran and started interpreting, the best she could, what the creature had said, but midway through her flow, she was interrupted—

'What's all this hand stuff?', the creature asked.

Fran explained. 'My brother, Bran, can't hear. We have this system back home where we can talk by making signs with our fingers.'

The creature looked puzzled. 'He can't talk? Not even head-to-head?'

Fran raised her eyebrows in surprise. 'What's head-to-head?'

'You know. You talk with your mind. It's safer when there are predators about. You can't be yelling "Ziggy! Ziggy! ZIGGY! WOLF ON YOUR LEFT!" in the middle of the night when you're about to be devoured.'

'That would be so cool, Bran!' Fran signed. 'Imagine if you could just say with your mind that you were frustrated with Miss Mackenzie during English rather than pulling that face you do. You'd get half the detentions.'

'Ahem,' the creature interrupted again. 'Head-to-head means you need to think AT me, not wave your hands at each other.'

Bran looked at the creature and thought with purpose, 'We have some questions. What's a Murder Fairy? And also, what kind of creature are you?'

'I'm a Zebracorn. I'm not a horse or a zebra or a unicorn, but a Zebracorn. We're unique to these parts. You don't see so many of us around these days, though, not since Prince Roger gave the order.'

Fran frowned and tried her own head-to-head (or heads, as both Bran and the Zebracorn seemed to have heard her). 'What order?'

The Zebracorn replied, in a booming, royalty-decree reading voice that rattled around their heads:

'For all magical creatures to be collected and

brought to be kept in his special zoo in the basement of the castle in Koto Utama.'

Fran froze. Then she bent down and picked up her mother's book.

'Did you say . . . Koto Utama?'

The Zebracorn nodded. 'Koto Utama. The magical royal city of this magical land. His Highness Prince Roger is trying to collect all the magic – including creatures – for himself. He says it's to keep the kingdom going, and as soon as he marries his new bride he'll return all the magic, but no one ever really returns the stuff they take, right? Especially not a meanie like Prince Roger. Ever since he took over, there's been more fancy parties and clothes and crowns at the palace and a whole lot less magic and food and stuff for us out here.'

The Zebracorn paused. 'He always looks *great* though, so I guess that's something.'

But Fran and Bran weren't paying attention. They stared at their mother's book. The book full of stories on the backs of envelopes, on napkins, and typed out with drawings contributed by Bran. The book called *The Tales of Koto Utama and the Nine Dominions.*

The Zebracorn waited for a few polite moments, and then said, 'So what are you doing? You don't look like you're from around here. You gotta be on a quest, right? That's it! You're on some life-or-death, wild-and-wonderful, fear-inducing kinda quest-type adventure, ain't you?'

Fran thought about the story she had just read, about the girl called Trouble, and begrudgingly admitted Bran was right about what Mum was trying to say. How having a magical creature on your quest was *always* a good thing. She turned to the Zebracorn. 'Kind of. Would you like to join us?'

The Zebracorn thought for a moment. 'I'm not sure. I have never been on a quest before. What are the hours like? Do I get rest breaks? Are meals included? What happens if my teeth fall out or I get sick? What exactly would my specific role on this quest be?'

Bran looked at Fran and signed, 'Perhaps it could carry us?'

Before Fran could answer, the Zebracorn holler rattled inside their heads,, 'HOLD UP! WAIT A MINUTE! I don't do transport – I have a very weak back. I might be able to ferry some light luggage, but you can forget about carrying you both. All the yoga in the world wouldn't be enough to fix my spinal column after that.' Bran interrupted. 'Wait, I thought you wouldn't understand us unless we thought AT you.'

'Oh I can,' the Zebracorn answered. 'But thinking AT someone is just polite.'

'All right,' thought Fran *politely*. 'So your role on our quest would be carrying light luggage.'

The Zebracorn nodded. 'OK. And what *is* this quest exactly?'

Fran and Bran thought for a moment. Then Bran explained, 'Our mother vanished in mysterious circumstances a few months ago. Everyone told us she must have died, but we think she wanted us to come here and find her. She left us clues in this book.' He nodded at the book Fran was clutching. 'See?'

The Zebracorn shrugged. 'Sounds likely enough to me.'

They put what little belongings they had on his

back and tied them down for balance. Then, with the Zebracorn leading the way, they headed down the undulating path through sharp-leafed woods. As they walked, they took it in turns to tell their stories.

'I'll start,' Zebracorn said chattily. 'I am part of an extraordinary species which is gifted with a number of skills. One of these is that I am a champion yarn-spinner. Do you know what that means?'

'No,' thought Fran, eyeing the path ahead anxiously.

'It means that I can tell amazing stories. My ancestors have won prizes in the Koto Utaman storytelling competition. You see, here in Koto Utama, stories are what keep the magic going, and magic is what keeps the stories going. And it's not just for us. The stories we come up with here become everyone's stories across the Nine Dominions and beyond . . .'

'Well that's . . . useful,' replied Bran, thinking that it might be more useful if the Zebracorn had been able to fly or turn grass into spaghetti.

'Correct! Because I'm the perfect Zebracorn to

document your quest. So what exactly are we doing? Fighting a dragon with bad breath? Waking a sleeping princess from a dream? Guessing a nasty pixie's name? I've got no thumbs or toes, so you can forget about me climbing a giant giggle-swanging beanstalk.'

Fran and Bran laughed. They weren't keen on climbing a giggle-swanging beanstalk either.

'Did you say you were trying to find your mom?'

'That's right. We've got to, or else we're going to be sent to some horrible posh boarding school.'

The Zebracorn had a shocked expression on his face. 'I don't know what that is, but I think you're very spoilt!'

Fran was stunned. 'That's a bit harsh, isn't it?'

The Zebracorn neighed and snorted. 'You come here to the most marvellous, magical kingdom of all to undergo a quest to avoid a *horrible posh boarding school.* Do you know what quests are? Do you know what they're for?'

'I'm not sure I see your point, Zebracorn,' Fran said, if a bit quietly.

'It's Zachary.'

'You never said.'

'You never asked.'

'We apologize.'

Zachary nodded. 'The point I'm making is that quests in the Nine Dominions – TRUE quests – aren't *just* about running away from something or even about finding someone. You should only be on a quest here if you want to fix something bad that's happened.'

Fran sighed. 'Well, our mum and dad going missing was pretty bad.'

Zachary shook his head.

Bran chimed in. 'There has to be a reason we are here and not somewhere else looking for our parents, right? Something that helps the whole kingdom?'

Zachary snorted once more, but this time more happily. 'They get the point, at last!'

And he did a little four-legged jig which involved several slalom-like effects with his hooves and little hitch-kicks which could have, if they had been any closer, taken someone's eye out.

Zachary settled into a companionable stroll and the twins walked alongside.

'But . . . how do we know what that reason is?' Fran asked. 'What kind of stuff around here needs fixing?'

'What kind of stuff doesn't? To even start answering that in full, I shall need hay and large chewy carrots and perhaps a turnip and some cold, clear stream water and a back rub, and later on a little canter without all this rubbish on my back . . .'

Bran felt he had to interrupt or Zachary would never stop talking. 'So, why do *you* think we're really here?'

But instead of answering, Zachary continued, 'Now, as it seems clear you don't know very much, let me explain. The Nine Dominions is a huge place. You got Koto Utama, the city with Mr Good-Looking Prince Roger the Handsome, who's thievin' magical creatures and is all excited cos he's gettin' married.

'Then you got Radnuuk, that's where most of the

Dark Elves live. If you don't like practical jokes, stay well clear of Radnuuk – they'll have you walkin' around with a sign that says KICK ME HARD all day long.

'Zaharda is chock-full of warrior people with horned helmets and enormous swords and for some reason they're always tellin' jokes.

'Then there's Giammica, which is teeming with wizards and witches and sorcerers and enchantresses. Giammica's mostly empty now cos all them magic folks have to go far afield and do lots of work these days since the Prince started taxing them too.

'Not to mention Deponya, which is where you are now. This is where we ordinary folk live, broke but still striving and surviving. Wait, did you meet the Mud Monster on your way here? Isn't he just adorable?'

Bran and Fran were struggling to take all this in. But Zachary continued, 'You say your mom's here? What's she look like?'

Bran answered first. 'She's the best mum in the

104

world, tells great stories, and doesn't mind you eating Pop-Tarts every day for a week for breakfast as long as you eat something green for lunch later in the day.'

Fran's reply was the same, but different. 'And she's an amazing storyteller. All of her stories are about a place called the Nine Dominions. It's a magical world filled with Vikings and elves and wizards.'

The Zebracorn stopped walking for a minute.

'Wait, your mother tells *stories* about Vikings and elves and wizards in a place called The Nine Dominions? What about Murder Fairies?'

Fran held up *The Tales of Koto Utama and the Nine Dominions*, which immediately flipped to a page entitled 'The Murder Fairies'. There was a scribbled story about how Murder Fairies got their names (It started off as a joke because their enemies thought they were all so titchy that they couldn't possibly defeat them in battle. Those enemies were soon staggering around thinking "Perhaps we underestimated those guys". Murder Fairies are the perfect of example of "Don't judge a book by its cover": especially if that book has armoured wings, an axe and a ferocious twinkle in its eye!)

The book flipped shut. The Zebracorn nodded his head. 'Interesting. What does your mother look like?'

The twins looked at each other. Fran started. 'She's got beautiful dark skin, big, curly hair, and she has gorgeous hazel eyes . . .'

Bran continued: 'She likes to wear lots of patterns and big colours because –' he and Fran glanced at each other and signed together their mother's favourite saying – 'no point leaving the house if someone hasn't said, "Wowsers, you look great!"'

Fran went on: 'She's got a laugh that makes everyone else laugh, and she's got a story about anything, anytime, anywhere, anyhow.'

Zachary was looking more and more thoughtful. 'Your mother is very dark-skinned, has big, curly hair, bright eyes, wears patterns and is an accomplished storyteller?'

They nodded. He looked them up and down. 'And you look to be approximately forty-eight seasons old.'

'We're twelve years old,' said Fran.

Zachary sighed. 'We measure age by seasons here. There are four seasons in your years, is that right? And you say you have twelve years, so . . .'

They did the maths. They were twelve, and if you did manage age by seasons, they would be forty-eight.

Fran wasn't sure where this was going but was starting to feel rude she hadn't asked anything more about Zachary. 'We haven't talked about you. How come you look like a spotty zebra but you've got a spike sticking out of your forehead?'

Zachary shrugged (Zebracorns can *absolutely* shrug – look it up). 'Zebracorns are half zebra, half unicorn, but because we're all mixed up we get treated like outcasts, misfits, rejects . . .'

Zachary looked really sad.

'But you're so beautiful and special,' Fran said.

'Yeah, you hear about boring old unicorns and horses all the time,' Bran agreed. 'I've never heard of anything as amazing as a Zebracorn. You're a rarity.'

Zachary's head came up and he strutted a little.

'Oh, I like that. Oh yes, a rarity. I am a rarity! Ha ha ha ha ha! A rarity, a . . .' He paused.

'What does *rarity* mean?'

Fran explained. 'It means you're rare, unique. There's not that many of you.'

On hearing that, Zachary once again looked sad. 'That's true,' he said. 'When I ride out nowadays I don't see any other Zebracorns any more. You almost never see a unicorn either. I told you, it's the stories that drive the magic, and we need magical creatures to be in the stories, so if Prince Roger has them all locked up . . . No creatures, no stories, no magic . . . We'll all disappear.'

'That's really sad,' said Fran. 'Maybe that's the thing we're here to help with.'

Zachary spun round six times and brayed as loud as a Zebracorn can. He reared up on his hind legs, and said five words that would change their lives from this moment on:

'YOU NEED A WIZARD GUIDE!'

CHAPTER ⑩

I n the meantime, at the palace, the Murder Fairies were holding a meeting.

Their leader was a gallant but sweaty commander called Zzzt (pronounced like *zeet*, but with more emphasis on the zeds) and he was in charge of the meeting. The subject of the meeting was: how had their kidnap of the much sought after Zebracorn been thwarted by two scrawny lookie-likie children?

The meeting space, which was more like a small cubbyhole if we're honest, was abuzz with commentary, complaint and caveats.

'I got hit in the face with a shovel.'

'I think the Zebracorn kicked me.'

'I think it was a spade, actually.'

'You were lucky it was just a kick. I was nearly kebabbed – it came *this* close.'

More grumbling filled the meeting space, and then a shadow fell across the room.

The regal presence of Prince Roger meant the buzzing Murder Fairies hovered to attention. They were all incredibly loyal, and believed firmly in their Prince.

The royal family dwelt at the very centre of the kingdom, surrounded by gorgeous woodlands and forests, with several stocks dotted here and there strategically for various villains, rapscallions and dunderheads to be put into and made an example of.

Nearer the town centre, and adjacent to the castle, were numerous souvenir shops which carried all manner of items, such as maps of the Nine Dominions sewn into silken blankets, framed and signed by the seamstress. There were engraved rings with inlaid pictures of royal babies from the past. There were silver-plate horseshoes and royal family portraits. But their bestselling items were paintings, brooches, devotional candles, boxer shorts, in fact *anything* with the handsome likeness of Prince Roger printed on them.

Or that's, at least, what the market-stall sellers told the Prince. In fact the market stalls ran a much more vibrant trade in potatoes and onions, the only food really available any more since Prince Roger started taxing just about everything else. You can forget the days of bartering a magic duck for some even more magical beans. These were desperate times – and besides, most magical artefacts, duck or otherwise, had been stashed in the capacious basement of the castle. Nowadays it was all about vegetables and cheap cuts of meat.

But however selfish he was, Prince Roger was still the only prince Koto Utama had, so he could have chosen anyone in the land to be his bride – but the only person he wanted for his wife was the Princess of the Dark Elves, one of the daughters of Chidozie, the sneakiest, wisest, most mischievous leader of the Dark Elves since the legendary Femi (who had once convinced a genie to give him unmatched wealth, the magnetic good looks of a matinee idol and, for his third and final wish, the capability to defeat any genie until the end of time).

A year and forty-eight seasons ago, the Prince had got his wish and become betrothed to Chidozie's daughter. A massive dowry had been paid: livestock, a cohort of Murder Fairies, sacred artefacts of magic, crates of gold, silver and jewels, a goose that laid golden eggs, and an ostrich the size of a house.

Prince Roger thought this was all very nice. But all he really wanted was her or – more importantly – her magic.

You see, she was made of it. If you were lucky enough to look closely at her skin or arms or pointed ears, you could almost see the sorcery glistening just under the surface.

The Prince didn't care too much for the Elven Princess herself, as beautiful and charming as she was. His First Chief Imperial Wizard (he was on number eighteen by now) told him they had worked out a way for him to capture her magic once they were married; a nefarious device had been constructed from the melted-down remains of various magical swords, lamps, fairy rings and precious stones – this now resembled a form of cannon, a hex-throwing howitzer, which could absorb every ounce of magic from whoever it was aimed at. Once he possessed her magic, he would be the most powerful Prince in all of the Nine Dominions and beyond.

But then everything had gone wrong. The Princess had slipped the net he had been so expertly weaving around her. It had been a dark time for the Prince, who, in order not to lose her dowry, (that gold did turn out to be handy) took it upon himself to write long, chatty letters in the guise of the Princess to her father, Chidozie. These letters usually began with copious respect and gratitude for marrying her off to such a handsome prince, and then proceeded to the far more important matters of fishing. Chidozie adored fishing, and had portraits of himself holding enormous sea creatures in his arms – sharks, dolphins, barracuda, and a baby Kraken. (Prince Roger was certain this last was a fake, but he wasn't brave enough to question an Elf Lord who would most certainly bring forces down upon his head if he found out his very beautiful and very beloved daughter had just disappeared into thin air . . .)

This was also a dark time for the First Chief Imperial Wizard, who was fired (because what good is a First Chief Imperial Wizard if he can't *set a guard to watch over a mere girl, magic or not, and keep her captive?*). The other massive (nay, enormous, nay, HUMUNGOUS) issue was the little matter of how the Nine Dominions relied on the Princess's storytelling magic to stay in general existence . . . Her disappearance, plus the Prince's greed, had brought hard times indeed.

Not that Prince Roger cared about any of *that*. He glared at the gathered Murder Fairies with royal contempt, and then spoke. 'No need to fill me in on what happened with the Zebracorn. It's all over the castle how you were bested by two orphans with shovels. No matter. I have been reliably informed by the Eighteenth Chief Imperial Wizard, Babadock, that the Princess has almost recovered from her transportation. Physically, that is; obviously she has no memory. Which is marvellous for us, because now all we have to do is make sure she doesn't escape again before *this* wedding. *Think we can manage that?'*

Zzzt saluted, which was followed by several hundred other snappy salutes from his underlings. He proffered a question. 'My Lord, I offer you my congratulations. What happens after the wedding? Tour of Nine Dominions, visiting your loyal public? Horse riding? Picking flowers? That sort of thing?'

Prince Roger smirked. 'Well, it's very nice of you to think of all those lovely activities for us. Sadly, the Princess will be an empty husk and destined for her grave within minutes of the magical transformation's completion. The wedding is this weekend, by the end of which yours truly will be the most powerful being in this or any other territory.'

He glared at the Murder Fairies with undisguised contempt in his eyes. 'Anyone who assists me in making my dreams come true will delight in my royal favour. Anyone else will find themselves as Chef's Special at the next Dwarf'n'Troll Barbecue Dinner and Dance! IS THAT UNDERSTOOD?'

Several hundred Murder Fairies saluted again, almost knocking themselves out in the process. With a sweep of his opulent jewel-encrusted cloak, Prince Roger left the room. As he walked down the corridor away from them, he couldn't help sniggering at how easy the Murder Fairies were to bully. But now that he knew that there were twin orphans with shovels on some kind of adventure quest, he had a sneaking suspicion that both of those shovels had his name on them.

For, it might just be a coincidence, but since his spies had informed him of the twins' presence, things had been *happening* all over the kingdom. Magical things.

In the nearby desert, a young lad called Ali had discovered a robber's cave filled with enchanted weaponry, gold and jewels.

The local pig-stealing musician's son, called Tom, was discovered hoarding enough salted pork meat in his larder to feed two villages for six months.

A cheeky girl had climbed the local beanstalk, stolen a magic duck that laid golden eggs, and slid back down the stalk like it was just everyday fun.

It might all just be a coincidence. But it made the Prince a touch nervous. He wiped his forehead with an ornately embroidered sleeve, and then yelled for his young Senior Wizard. The transformation ceremony would happen in two days' time and they must hire the best mercenaries in the Nine Dominions as security. Nothing, or no one, could disrupt the ritual, and if they did . . .

But there the Prince lost his train of thought because he had passed a mirror and caught sight of himself, and almost fainted from the sheer handsomeness of it all.

'Your Highness?'

The wizard Babadock, who had seen this many times before, cleared his throat and said more loudly, 'Your Highness?'

Prince Roger blinked several times, and then stared at Babadock as if he were a giraffe wearing a tuxedo.

'Ah, Babadock, we're getting very close to the

wedding and the transformation. Is everything in order?'

'Yes, Your Highness. The apparatus for the transformation ritual has been erected in the palace grounds. The locals have been invited to witness the ceremony and I've sent an order to the Bloodsword Chieftains to act as our security force for the day.'

The Prince looked at Babadock quizzically. 'Did you tell them we have no money? I can't give them anything until I am possessed with magic, and then I'll be able to pull gold coins from my ears and silver ones from my nose, not only that, I shall yank diamonds from my—'

'I was vague about the money, Your Highness.'

The Prince nodded. 'Good, good. How *are* the royal accounts?'

Babadock retrieved a notebook from within the folds of his gown, which was emblazoned with the royal logo. He flipped pages for quite a long time. Prince Roger tapped his jewel-encrusted slipper impatiently. Babadock kept flipping until he got to the end of this book. He shook his head. Prince Roger snatched the notebook from him, stared at the page, then looked up and glared at Babadock.

'What are all these zeros?'

The wizard shrugged. 'That's what our accounts look like.'

'We're *completely* broke? There's *nothing*? What about all the taxes I've been raising?'

'Fifty-two seasons ago you drained our coffers to

woo the Princess,' the wizard explained patiently. 'And everything that comes in, including the princess's dowry all those years ago, goes straight back out . . .' Babdock gestured to Prince Roger's very impressive bejewelled cloak. 'That's why I can't pay staff or trainee wizards, or any of our bills. That's why the windows are dirty, the larders are empty, the toilets unflushed, your shirts are unironed, your collars unstarched, and your koi carp are parched—'

The Prince scowled. 'As soon as the Princess and I are married, her powers will become mine, I will become the most powerful being in all the lands, and no one will be bothering me about bills ever again! Have I made myself clear?'

He stormed off with a sweep of his voluminous cloak.

Babadock looked troubled. He had also heard about shovel-wielding, book-carrying twins. If those children were who he thought they might be . . . well, then the Prince's carefully laid plans were all about to sail up the shark-infested creek in a leaky canoe with no paddle.

CHAPTER

While all this was happening, the Princess lay in a chamber, deep within Koto Utama Castle. She had arrived one night wearing a large raincoat, with a roll of loo paper in one hand (the soft kind, not the shiny stuff that didn't actually *do* anything) and a book in the other (*The Lion, the Witch and the Wardrobe* – just in case she wanted to read for a while).

Now all of these things had gone. She lay on a luxurious royal bed, wearing a silken nightdress; her hair had been conditioned and plaited, and her skin moisturized. She couldn't shake the feeling (even though she was in the midst of a particularly deep sleep) that she *knew* this place. She was also aware that she needed to save herself.

Her magic was a natural thing that she spun from a tapestry of wit, invention, imagination, spit and sawdust. And she knew that if she didn't come up with something soon – something spectacular, something so mind-bogglingly, eye-gogglingly clever, that even the most learned of professors would look at her and the magic she wrought and say to each other 'My word, that *is* clever!' – then she would never make it out of this chamber alive.

As the sky over Koto Utamu pinked and purpled, winging its way to darkling night, she pursued a double-edged dream that was not only a story in its own right, but also a lesson that she wanted to pass on to two people in particular.

She hit the sweet spot of the dream where characters and meaning and theme and conclusions bubbled, steamed and sizzled like a particularly delicious stew. She drifted through dreamland but if she had been awake, she might have clapped her hands with pleasure and said, 'Wowsers!'

Yemi and the
Reason for Living

Yemi was from a village called Digeris. Yemi was on a special quest because Digeris was dying.

He decided to travel to the sacred temple where an ancient wizard lived. When Yemi arrived at the temple, he found the wizard working in his garden.

'Excuse me,' Yemi said. 'With great respect, I approach in the full knowledge that your time is of untold value and that you do not dispense your skills thoughtlessly or without consideration. However, and needless to say, I would not be here if I did not humbly and desperately need your assistance.'

The old wizard shook his head. 'I can't help you,' he said. 'Ever since my wife died, I work in my garden and that's it.'

But Yemi, even though he sympathized with the old man's grief pleaded with him.

'My village is starving. Most of the men went off to Zhardza to join the warriors there. The children are too small and the women are tired. There is just myself, Aku and Barruk, and we are not funny or strong enough to be Viking warriors. They require the specific qualifications of an encyclopaedic collection of jokes and the ability to lift a fully grown horse without breaking into a sweat. We are not enough to do all the planting by ourselves. Winter will soon be here, and if we do not harvest the crops in time, my family and everybody else's family will die, and . . .'

He trailed off, realizing that the wizard wasn't listening. Instead, he was busy sowing seeds, pushing them down into the rich, dark earth. He wiped his hands on his overalls and asked, 'Yemi, what exactly do you want from me?'

Yemi wiped sweat from his brow. 'O wise one, I would ask that you be of assistance to the people of my village. We need *magical* assistance. Because alone we cannot . . .'

Yemi trailed off again. The wizard was busily deadheading brightly coloured flowers now, and ignoring him completely.

'Yemi, if you don't get to the point, I will wither and die like these yams.'

Yemi tried one more time. 'Ancient, yet powerful one, if I were to pick up a shovel here and help you with your garden, would you help us with our crops and future harvest? We would be eternally grateful.'

WHAM! A shovel landed at Yemi's feet, and the wizard pointed at some potatoes.

'Have a dig around there, Yemi, and see if you can't pick out the good from the bad. You should think about this in regard to your message-giving. Just like those plums over there, your messages could do with some pruning.'

And lo, Yemi stayed with the old wizard for weeks, planting, pruning, digging, cultivating and landscaping.

Then, one day, tired from all the work, he simply said, 'Please help my people now.'

And with that, the wizard fetched a strong cart with powerful wooden wheels. He filled the cart with shovels, hoes, rakes, a variety of seeds, vegetables, powders, fertilizers and smelly manure. He beckoned for Yemi to sit at the front, behind two of the largest horses he had ever seen. Then he said, 'Which way?'

Yemi pointed towards his village near the mountain. And with that the wizard clapped his hands three times and the horses took to the sky and flew speedily to the village, touching down in the main square.

On arrival, the wizard asked if anyone wanted to help, and all the children and the women and Aku and Barruk said yes. Then the wizard said, 'Yemi, why don't you begin?'

And for the next short while Yemi directed them all with everything he had learned from the wizard's garden. As they mapped out and marked, ploughed and planted, deadheaded and dug, there was joyous music too, and they sang as they sowed and seeded.

The wizard listened carefully to all of this, and once the landscaping and planting had been done, he said, 'This is a very fertile ground. From now on, your harvests will be excellent.'

Yemi started to say, 'Thank you.'

But the wizard shook his head to stop Yemi. 'There is no need to thank me. You saved your own village.'

So the morals of the story, children, are that you can give a man a fish, but it is perhaps better to teach a man to fish. That if you want to ask a favour, true need doesn't need flowery words. And, also that wizards are much sneakier than they look.

The End

CHAPTER

The children had woken that morning after a troubled and uncomfortable night spent on the forest floor where they had dreamed of wizards and planting and singing. They were both filled with a strange sense of urgency.

'It feels like time is running out for our quest,' Fran signed.

'I know,' Bran replied. 'Like we only have a couple days left.'

Zachary was wide awake too, and full of beans – and clearly listening. 'Coincidentally, there's only a couple days left before the royal wedding. I want to be there. Gonna have a cake the size of a cow and I'm gonna get me a piece of that.'

He stretched, and then set off cantering at such a clip that Bran and Fran were having to half run to keep up.

'Come on!' he hollered. 'We don't have very long! Let's go find our wizard!'

Fran wasn't so sure. 'I'm worried about the wizard thing,' she said.

Bran couldn't believe it. 'You're not backing out of this, are you? We *need* a wizard. Don't you want to have an adventure?'

Fran took great exception to this. '*Of course* I want an adventure. I just don't want to get squished by a giant or devoured by a dwarf or fricasseed by a Fire Lizard—'

Bran signed that she should take a minute, breathe deeply in for ten, and out for ten. She did this for two minutes and found that she had calmed down considerably.

She signed at her brother, 'Where'd you learn that?'

He signed back, 'Madge has been practising her

deep-breathing exercises ever since I put superglue on the fridge door.'

His sister laughed and they set off at a trot.

'How are we going to get a wizard to help us?' Fran asked as they cantered along, trying to keep up with Zach.

'Why wouldn't he help us?' Bran signed back.

'We don't have any money. So we'll have to convince him we're on a super-important quest.' Fran started practising. 'O great wizard, will you help us lowly questers on our, um, questing . . .'

Bran snorted. 'You're gonna have to grovel better than that,' he signed.

'I thought that was good.'

'*Lowly questers*? You've got a screw loose.'

This argument went on, with the odd break for hay, snack, water, or a wee behind the tree, for hours.

Zachary beamed at them. 'I have to say, you both did very well. Keeping up with a Zebracorn all day is not easy.' He tilted his head and looked at them. 'Yes. There's definitely something about you two.'

Fran slumped. 'I just want to find Mum, that's all. And if we have to find a wizard first—'

Bran interrupted to sign he was tired and if he didn't get some rest soon, he was going to head-to-head scream at them for an hour and a half.

'You're in luck,' said Zachary. 'We're just outside the wizards' dominion of Giammica.'

They walked and observed just how run-down and raggedy this particular area was. Zachary had a good look round and observed, almost to himself, 'I haven't been to Giammica in some time, but this place looks like the maid quit last year and they are too broke to get another one . . .'

Clearly the wizards were also hurting from Prince Roger's magic-stealing and taxes. They took in the formerly grandiose and gorgeous dwellings as they walked down the main road.

There was a small castle with a black marble dragon on its roof. Zachary advised them to steer clear of that one.

'Obsidian, the wizard, is said to have killed this

beast and devoured its heart to absorb its power. Let's not go anywhere near him.'

Bran asked hesitantly, 'Is he an evil wizard?'

'Nah,' replied Zachary. 'He's a pussycat. But have you ever tasted dragon? His breath stinks.'

They moved on until they reached an incredibly scruffy dwelling: a patchwork barn supported by sticks and planks and bits of thatch near a large pond. There was an enormous and fierce-looking fish creature painted on the front door.

The Zebracorn indicated with his head. 'Now that's the wizard Carperian. He's said to be related to the sea god Piscaton. Not much use to us if we're inland. Keep going.'

The next house was made of rock and stone, with a small live volcano in the front garden. Fran and Bran were very impressed, but Zachary gestured at them to hurry past. 'Do you two want your eyebrows melted off? Flipping flip, this is Ephos's house.'

Suddenly there was a puff of smoke and orange lava poured down the sides of the volcano.

'Who is Ephos?' asked Fran.

'The great wizard Ephos travelled for a year and a day to the vicious volcano to dispatch the lightning wizard, Shastos, who was hell-bent on destroying the world. He won't be here. He's one of the most in-demand warlocks in the Nine Dominions,' Zachary explained.

Just then, there was a mighty explosion. The volcano erupted once more, and a large trunk flew from inside Ephos's front door. It was then followed by a tall, dreadlocked man wearing robes and sandals and just about clutching a big stick, which snapped in two as he landed and then reassembled itself in order to help him up.

From inside, a voice yelled, 'That's right, Ephos. Do what you always do. Run away. I don't care.'

Ephos brushed grass and dust stains from his robes and yelled back, 'Maybe I *wouldn't* keep going off and having adventures with my friends if you were just a little bit nicer . . .'

A dreadlocked woman in robes came storming out

of the house. Her skin was nut brown, her forearms resplendent with ornate tattoos, her ears were elvishly pointed – and her eyes flashed with tears.

'You – you – you – you – you – NINCOMPOOP!' she spluttered. 'How dare you blame me! I didn't ask you to marry me. You wooed me. And the second we were married, you tell me you're needed urgently by the dwarves to defeat the evil God of Fear from beneath the great mountain, and that was you gone for *four years*! And now you want to leave again!'

'Let's go,' said Fran. 'This feels like a private conversation.'

'No,' said Zebracorn. 'He's a great wizard. And we need a great wizard.'

He raised his voice. 'I understand that this may not be the best moment to interrupt, but these children need your help. They are on a quest!'

'Ooh, a quest,' said Ephos, perking up. 'I do like a quest.'

The woman let out a howl of rage. 'You people are all the same! You don't want to go on a quest to conquer evil – you just want to get out of the house!'

She turned her back and returned to the confines of her home, slamming the door behind her. The volcano emitted a tiny *plip* noise.

Ephos sighed. 'She's always like this. She doesn't want me to live my best life.'

He twisted his waist-long locks into a cone that sat neatly on the top of his head and then encased them with a pointy hat of silver and gold.

'I'd love to help you with your quest, honestly I would,' he said. 'But I'm needed elsewhere. Try Mystos down the road. He is the one with that vicious green snake statue on his roof. He's a sweet chap. Or –' he gestured towards a Gothic-style abode, swarming with bats in its belfry – 'you could try Louella Demone.'

'OK . . .' said Fran. 'Because we really do need a wizard.'

Ephos looked at them. 'Listen, I get it. You want someone with the power to actually do something for you. But don't forget you also have to do some brave things for yourself or you won't learn anything. That's the whole point of going on a quest.'

He paused and watched Zachary for a moment, cropping tall grass under the trees.

'Nice Zebracorn, by the way. You don't see many of those guys any more.'

And then he picked up his case and took his trunk

and strapped it to his chest, grabbed his staff, tapped the ground three times and disappeared in a lurch and a wobble and a *ping*. It was as though he had never been there.

Bran was smiling and signing at the same time. 'That was awesome. Where shall we try next?'

Fran shook her head. 'Bran, that wasn't awesome. That lady was really upset.'

And without really thinking what she was doing, she walked up to the lady's door. There was a home-made plaque attached to a wooden post which said *Gone Warlocking*. She knocked again and the door whammed open as if it had a grudge.

The woman stood looking at them all with tearful eyes. She seemed smaller now than when she was outside yelling at Ephos.

'Hi,' she said. 'I don't suppose anyone wants a cup of tea, do they?'

CHAPTER 13

They followed her into the house. 'Please, take a seat,' said the wizard's wife. 'I'll go and put the kettle on.'

Fran and Bran looked at each other. From the outside, the house resembled a relatively small bungalow, but inside there was a sizeable oak tree growing through the centre of the large, warm kitchen. A living room the size of a five-a-side football pitch was festooned with dramatic statues of Ephos in battle with a Minotaur, Ephos with his wand raised as a giant tried to stomp him like a bug, and Ephos wielding a fighting staff standing at the edge of a smashed bridge with a carved caption underneath that said: *Go Back or Mi Wi' Bus' Yu Head!*

And on the walls there were huge paintings depicting ages-old battle scenes, which as they watched, kept *changing* to give another point of view or a close-up of events as they happened. The whole house was like this.

'Cool,' signed Bran.

'Wowsers,' signed Fran.

'Yes,' agreed Zachary. 'And I am most excited about this cup of tea.'

Fran turned to him. 'Zachary. Do you know what a cup of tea is?'

Zachary looked indignant. 'Of course I do! I can't wait till she brings me my tea. I wonder how big it will be? Will she bring it in an enormous box? Or will it just be in her hand? Tea. It sounds so mysterious. A special potion, perhaps. I wonder whether it will make my coat more lustrous. My mane more silky . . .'

Bran looked at his sister, trying not to laugh. 'He has no idea what tea is, does he?'

Fran replied, 'Clueless.'

She turned back to the Zebracorn. 'Zachary, tea is a drink. It's flavoured with leaves that turn it brown and sort of bitter. And then you can put milk or sugar or sometimes both in it.'

The Zebracorn recoiled in horror. 'Leaves? Bitter leaves with milk? That sounds like the most disgusting thing I have ever heard. Tell you what, I'll wait outside. Just be sure to think loudly if anything important happens.'

He tossed his mane and strutted out of the house as if he had been grossly insulted.

Fran and Bran were still laughing when the wizard's wife arrived with the tea tray. There was a large, intricately carved teapot. Bran looked closely and could see detailed carvings of winged creatures, pointy-eared animals, tiny human-type creatures with swords, and some replendent trees that tied the whole design together.

'It's beautiful,' he signed.

The wizard's wife sniffed and signed back, 'Dwarven silver. *He* brought this home for me from one of his travels. He says it's quite valuable. Whatever Ephos says, I've never had a bad cup of tea out of it, so it can't be all that bad.'

When Bran and Fran's eyes went wide, she looked at them and shrugged. 'My big sister Elizabeth is deaf.' With that, she made the tea and a tray of sandwiches was set down. There were small plates, each one with a caricature painted onto them. When Bran looked at his plate, he was gobsmacked.

Bran signed, 'This looks just like me.'

It did. There was Bran's shock of curly hair and bright, inquisitive eyes.

Fran looked at her plate and, once again, the caricature looked like her. Whoever had done the drawing was very clever.

'How did you do this?' Bran asked excitedly.

Their host shrugged. 'My Elven crockery has got all kinds of tricks up its sleeve.'

Fran looked around. 'Is *everything* in this house magic?'

Bran shook his head and signed, 'What kind

of question is that? She's married to a wizard, you numpty.'

Fran shot back, 'Don't call me a numpty.'

'Well, you are a numpty.'

'I know you are, but what am I?'

Zachary put his head through an open window. 'This lady has gone out of her way to make stinky bush tea with hot water and some kind of disgusting milk. The least you could do is be still for a moment and pretend to like it.'

His head disappeared back through the window.

The wizard's wife looked at them both. 'So you're on a quest, is that right?'

Fran nodded. 'We wanted to ask the wizard, your husband, for help, but it looks like he's gone.'

'My son is a wizard too. He's gone as well.' The wizard's wife sighed. They thought she was going to start crying again. 'Well, why don't you try asking me? My name is Wilma, by the way. I'm Ephos's wife, but not for much longer if he keeps treating me like this. It's time I do something for myself – like help you!' She seemed to brighten a little. 'I've got what it takes. Used to be able to best the lot of them, back in the day. So what's our quest?'

Bran began to sign the whole thing at furious speed. It all poured out of him in a jumble. Dad gone, Mum gone, the threat of boarding school, the Murder Fairies, Zachary the Zebracorn, and Mum's brilliant book of stories that might or might not be giving them clues.

Wilma said, 'How did your mum and dad go missing?'

Fran picked up the story. 'They both disappeared in a flash of lightning. Our Auntie Madge wants us to go to this boarding school up north. We just want to find our mum – well, both our parents really – and go home.'

Zachary poked his head through the open window again.

'Ahem. What about helping out the Nine Dominions? What about that?'

'Yes, of course,' Fran quickly added. 'Zachary says

that quests usually involve helping people other than yourself. So we thought we could save the magical creatures and defeat the evil Prince or . . . something.'

Wilma nodded. 'And how old did you say you were?'

'Why does everybody keep asking us that?' Bran signed. 'We're twelve.'

'Or forty-eight seasons,' Fran clarified, remembering how age worked in this magical land.

Wilma looked at Zachary, who had returned to his place and was resting his chin on the windowsill. They exchanged a long glance.

'Right,' she said suddenly. 'You need to eat up because you're going to need all your strength. If I know anything from what Ephos tells me about quests, it's that they are fraught with danger. The minute whoever's being quested against finds out they are being quested at, they begin an anti-quest. This is where the questors suddenly discover that the questees have sussed out what's going on and are now determined not to be stopped mid-quest from achieving whatever *they* are questing for.'

Then she leapt to her feet. 'We'll need the Impossible Map and some food and drink. Now do you think your friend, the Zebracorn, would like some hay? I'm sure we have got some somewhere. I'll pack a bag. Please use the facilities before you leave, children.'

For the next half-hour, the kids watched open-mouthed as Wilma packed. The more things she placed in her (accurately named) Hold-All bag, the more the bag would grunt, jiggle about momentarily, puff itself

out, and then return to its regular size, ready to receive more items.

'She's a clever old bag when it comes down to it.' Wilma winked.

As a last flourish Wilma pulled out a large piece of parchment and a beautiful quill. As she spoke, the quill pen dipped its point into the ink and began independently writing a particularly venomous message for her husband.

Ephos,

I would have written 'Dear Ephos', but I don't feel 'dear' to you any more. You'd rather spend all your time away from me. And, for the first time ever in our marriage, I am taking action. From now on I shall do what I want to do because I want to do it. I refuse to twiddle my thumbs like some mooning castle maiden frittering her best years away whilst you quest to your heart's content.

You'll be surprised to know that I've been asked to take up a dangerous quest of my own.

I do still care for you, but if it's hot where you are, I hope your nostril hairs ignite on an hourly basis. If it's cold, I pray that your feet become icicles and your ears turn blue.

I have taken the liberty of borrowing a few of your things for my journey. These are all things you left behind, so you obviously don't need them. Besides, we have been married for 140 seasons  and half of this rubbish is mine anyway. Just so you know, I've taken: your old wand, the Impossible Map of Possibilities and the seven-league boots, all eight pairs.

If I'm not here when you get back, tough.

Signed, rather crossly,

Wilma (your wife, remember?)

With that she ushered them out of the little house. There was a goat grazing the lawn outside and they loaded it up with bags, sticks, artefacts, food, spare shoes, rain cloaks and hoods, and a large wheel of white cheese that resembled Brie, but probably wasn't.

Fran said, 'I'm glad we're taking your goat. Zachary is not really built for being a beast of burden.'

'Too right,' said Zachary.

Wilma laughed and waved her newly acquired wand at the house, which suddenly grew copious amounts of grass on its every available surface. It sprouted bushes and small trees and exotic-looking flowers and a plethora of plants, which neither Fran, nor Bran, nor Zachary recognized. Soon the house resembled a gorgeous mound of flora in the middle of a bunch of wizard houses. It was as if Ephos's house had never been there.

They began to walk.

'Um . . .' Fran started. 'Where are we going?'

But before anyone could answer, the skies opened up.

CHAPTER 14

They had been walking for hours in the pouring rain. Bran and Fran bickered the entire time. Bran kept complaining, 'This is boring.'

Fran would reply, 'There's always a bit in adventures that are boring. But in the books they cut this bit out.'

Bran kicked a pebble. 'They shouldn't do that. They should warn you that it's going to be mind-numbingly, brain-achingly, stomach-churningly dull sometimes. I bet if Gandalf had told Bilbo Baggins that there were going to be long stretches of the adventure where they just kept walking through mud and rabbit poo and not having a decent meal for hours on end, Bilbo would have said "Ooh, actually I think

I'll just stay at home instead and wait for the movie with those bits edited out.'''

'You're impossible.' Fran shook her head. 'But right.'

She turned to Zachary. 'Can we have a break pleeeeease?'

Zach wrinkled his nose. 'What kind of a break? Is this a summer break? A weekend break? A break in your neck or foreleg? A break in concentration? Come on, out with it. Be specific.'

Fran gathered her thoughts for a second and briefly contemplated Madge's breathing exercises. 'We'd like a *rest* break. Our feet hurt. We need the loo, and perhaps a biscuit and a cup of tea. And maybe we could discuss the plan a bit more?'

Zachary pulled a face. 'What *is* it with you two and this tea?'

Wilma looked back at Bran, trudging dejectedly along, Zachary head-to-head chatting away at his side. She couldn't quite make out what the Zebracorn was saying from this far away (head-to-head had the same distance limits as regular speech) but she could tell it was getting annoying.

'All right,' said Wilma. 'Let's have a break.'

With that decision made, Wilma tied the goat, whose name was Nelson, to a tree, and took down her bag of wonders. From it she produced a folding table, three chairs, an elaborately decorated chocolate cake, some oatmeal-and-raisin cookies, three self-replenishing mugs of tea (Elvish-made, they stop refilling only when you tell them to) and a large bale of hay with acorns on the side for Zachary.

Bran eyed the chocolate cake greedily and proceeded to carve a slab the size of a small bungalow just for himself. By now, Fran was on her second oatmeal-and-raisin cookie and sipping at her piping hot tea. Wilma was delicately picking at a bowl of homemade granola.

As Bran tucked into the chocolate cake, he started signing to Fran. He always did this at meal times It was one of their jokes, that he *could* talk with his mouth full. He chewed as he signed, 'So, what's the plan, Stan?'

Wilma blinked. 'Stan?'

'It's an expression,' said Fran. 'Where are going?'

'What do you mean, "Where are we going"?' Wilma asked.

'We only knew to go as far as to find a wizard,' Bran signed.

'We mean you,' Fran quickly corrected.

'You're on a quest with no idea of where you're questing to?' Wilma harrumphed. 'Amateurs!' She sighed, and pulled out a map.

'This might help. It is the Impossible Map of Possibilities. Everywhere you see a glowing red dot is possibly an impossible task. My husband won it in a poker game from Mgaaabe. His breath was rancid and he never cut his toenails, but his map has proven very useful.'

Wilma made room on the table for the map, and they all peered at it. On it were all of the Nine Dominions – the mountains, streams, rivers, oceans, fortresses, villages, castles, chip shops, encampments.

'Now, here is the Viking camp in Zaharda, home of the Bloodswords.' Wilma pointed at a large, glowing red dot on an otherwise very lovely and well-drawn

map. 'That looks like one very BIG impossible possibility. And here, at the castle in Koto Utama, is the other. It's not quite as bright, so I think we have approximately two days before it possibly becomes a real problem.'

'Two days . . .' signed Fran slowly. 'Wait – that's when the royal wedding is! Could that be important? Maybe we should go and investigate.'

'But what about the big glowing red dot in the Viking's land?' Bran's expressive fingers argued. 'Something is happening there now!'

'*Something*, yes. But why would Mum be with the Vikings? We're just getting distracted, Bran.'

'You're both right,' Wilma explained. 'It's showing

us the possibilities as well as what's actually there. So there's an equally good chance you're either needed or not needed in both places at the same time. Which isn't possible unless you split up.'

'That's impossible,' Fran quickly signed.

At the same time, Bran signed, 'OK.'

Nelson, the goat, dropped fourteen pellets from his rear end.

Zachary looked up from his enormous, half-eaten hay bale and shuddered. 'You really mean it, Bran? You want to split up? As in, "You go your way and I'll go mine"? As in, "I'll keep the castle, you take the swimming pool, six horses, the contents of your wardrobe, including all them shoes, and I'll take the summer house by the river, the kids, and the trunk of gold bars you don't know about in the basement. Have your people send over the paperwork cos we're done and dusted"?'

The twins looked at each other. Bran rolled his eyes. 'I think I grew a beard while he was talking.'

Fran laughed and replied, 'I just watched every season of *Dr Who*, even the old ones in black and white, in my mind while he was saying all that.'

Then she got serious. 'We're not splitting up. There's a reason you put a gang together when you're having an adventure like this. It's because everybody has a skill to get the gang out of trouble and so they stick together to make sure they can take advantage of all those skills.'

Wilma shook her head. 'Sticking together is great if you're a regiment attacking a fortress. Or a synchronized swimming team. But in this instance, splitting up might be better.

You two will each need someone who knows the territory, so Fran and I will do the tough bit and Bran and Zach can do the easy bit.'

Bran's fingers were a blur. 'What do you mean, the tough bit? I'm not scared. Where's the tough bit?'

Wilma tapped the glowing red spot that was the Viking encampment. 'Probably battling a battalion of blood-thirsty warriors with notoriously bad jokes.'

Bran exploded. 'That's the stupidest thing I've ever heard. Boys are supposed to be brave – they're the ones who are always knights in stories.'

'Really?' said Fran, raising an eyebrow. 'And what do the girls do?'

'Um . . . they bandage up the knights when they're injured,' said Bran.

Wilma blinked. 'Where *did* you get these ideas from?' she said.

'Well,' signed Bran rather weakly. 'From all the stories.'

'Not Mum's stories,' Fran countered.

Wilma gave his arm a pat. 'In *this* story the girls and the boys do something different,' she said.

Fran waved her hands at the map. 'Look! That blob has changed.'

Everyone stopped and stared. Something *had* changed. The second spot was now glowing bright red too, and blinking on and off intermittently like a faulty traffic light.

Wilma drew in a sharp breath. 'It looks like storming the castle is an equally dangerous mission now. Who'd have thunk it?'

Bran grinned. 'Now we're talking.'

'But I should be there to help you,' said Fran.

'You need me—'

'No.' Bran cut her off. 'I can do some things on my own.'

The twins were silent for a second.

'Do I get any say in if I go *at all*?' Zach said.

'I'm afraid not,' Wilma said. 'You're a creature of magic. I need you to watch out for one of these human children. Although I have no idea what it is you actually do, magic-wise.'

Bran patted Zachary's head. 'We'll be fine. We should disguise ourselves, though. We stand out a bit.'

Zachary looked a little happier. 'I like the idea of a disguise. Maybe I could be a rock or a tree? Something that doesn't move and doesn't go anywhere dangerous.'

Fran laughed. 'Shall we have one of Mum's stories before we go?'

Bran signed that he thought this was a good idea. (Which was pretty much twin language for 'You're right' and 'I'm sorry too'.) At that moment, the book opened itself and its pages fluttered until it landed on the story of the River Twins.

The River Twins and What They Learned

Sami and Dumay were brother and sister. They lived in a remote village on the outskirts of the Whaderar dominion.

Their village was nestled next to a flowing river that was packed full of jumping fish that practically leapt into the fishermen's nets. Even though in other dominions people were suffering through lack of food and trade for their skills, in this village, which was called Edadkre, people shared their food and clean water, they looked out for each other, and everyone thrived.

Dumay was made to work with her aunties and mother and cousins. The kitchen garden was always busy with people

picking leaves to ease
constipation, headaches,
or to get rid of bad breath; in
the kitchen they pounded pestle
and mortar to make pastes to heal
cuts and bruises. The women passed
on their knowledge to Dumay, and she told
Sami everything she'd learned at the end of every day.

Sami was made to go out into the forest, hunting and
fishing and hacking down trees and then chopping those
into logs. He was strong for his age but found all this
hunting and hacking tedious. He also had to practise
sword fighting every day for two hours. The swords
were heavy and had incredibly sharp blades that could
slice the end from a flea's left eyebrow.

Sami was always exhausted at the end of the day,
but before supper he would never fail to take the time to
show Dumay what he had learned, whether it was how
to wriggle your way out of a neck lock, or how to slice
the toenails from a passing dragonfly.

In return, Dumay would show him what she had learned in the gardens, pointing out the herbs and berries and explaining what they did.

One day, the Oorlogz, a warlike people who shaved their heads and cultivated muscles and wore gaudy tattoos (the men were like this too) decided to attack Edadkre. Their spies had watched for years as the people of Edadkre quietly fished in the river, raised cattle and crops, and built a beautiful habitat for their people. The Oorlogz were jealous and wanted what they didn't have.

The Edadkre men were caught unawares. Although they were strong and capable fighters, there hadn't been an attack on their village for some time and they had grown complacent.

Dumay was out in the herb gardens with her mother, aunties and sisters. When they saw the soldiers suddenly appear on their side of the river, everyone else screamed and ran to the hills. But Dumay sped to the place where all the swords were kept and, with one in each hand, set out to take on the attackers.

Half the Oorlogz cohort stood in front of her now on the path to the compound, and she shouted at them, 'Which one of you wishes defeat from a mere girl?'

Dumay knew there was no such thing as a 'mere girl', especially not one that had trained like her. But the Oorlogz laughed, and their first in command, Doogz, who was completely tattooed from head to foot, with one solo braid of hair from the middle of his bald head, stepped up to her, drew his sword and sneered.

'I shall skewer you like a side of beef!'

And he rushed at her, his sword whirling and flashing silver in the sunlight.

Dumay completely humiliated him. She spun like a dervish, easily defending herself. She batted and swatted and kicked and punched with expert ease until Doogz was not only exhausted but scared. If this small girl was such a fierce fighter, what was the rest of the village like?

'She's dangerous,' Doogz yelled to his warriors.

'Let's run away!' Half the invading Oorlogz ran back to the river.

The minute the sounds of the epic battle of Dumay and Doogz reached the ears of everyone back at the compound, they knew there was an attack coming. Sami's father, uncles and cousins decided the best thing to do was to lock all the children safely behind the heavy doors of the kitchen, pile rocks against them, and then head for a vantage point up the hill and have a long meeting about what to do next. This strategy is called 'Running Away'.

But Sami, rather than feel frightened or sad, had a different plan. He decided that he and the other children would cook a magnificent feast for the Oorlogz. He made a special herbal rub for the cow meat and began frying enough steaks for a small army. He asked his cousins and brothers and sisters and friends to help him prepare vegetables and fruit – all of which were sprinkled with Sami's special combination of herbs.

The doors of the kitchen smashed open. It had taken a

while for the second half of the Oorlogz forces to remove the heavy rocks, but, driven by the irresistible smell of delicious food, they were now through.

The soldiers sat at tables and waited as the herby fried steaks and vegetables came out in a multicoloured parade of delicious offerings.

The Oorlogz ignored the children as they ate and ate. Sami had never seen such appetites. Inevitably, the eating and drinking came to an end – and every single soldier at the dining table looked full to bursting, their lips greasy with steak fat, and their stomachs bulging. They were happy and satisfied.

And then Loogz, the Oorlogz second in command, began burping.

BURP! BURRRRPPP! BURRRRRRRRRRRP!

His deputy started retching – HUAK! HUAAAKAAA! HUBUUUUYAAAKKKAAAAA!

And he himself made a noise with his bottom that had to be heard to be believed:

PAAARP! PAAAARP! RAAPGPGPGPGPAPA-

APAPAPAPAPAPAPAAAAAAAAAAAAAARP!

And soon all the soldiers were burping, retching and parping. The noises combined made them all sound like a bizarre brass band. They cried tears of pain as their bellies betrayed them.

PAAARAAAPPPAAAARRRRAPPPPAAAARP!

And this is when Edadkre's soldiers descended from the nearby hills and down upon the enemy and bonked them on their heads, tied them in a net and sent them packing back to their own village, warning them that if they could be defeated so easily by children, just imagine the damage their parents and elders could do.

Dumay and Sami were declared heroes, and proved that if you work together and pass on what you know, you can solve any problem.

The End

Fran closed the book and looked around at them all. Zachary looked a bit sick.

'That was pretty gross,' he muttered.

'Look, Mum must have put this story in here for a reason,' Bran said. 'I think she wants us to realize how important it is to learn things from each other.'

'Or she's trying to tell us that sticking together is the only way, and we're foolish to split up,' Fran replied quietly.

Wilma was busy packing away the food, but paused to raise her hands and contribute. 'Or she's advising us that we're going to need an army to help us overcome what's ahead. I think, if you can persuade the leader of the Bloodswords to follow you into battle and be our reinforcements, then we could turn things around.'

'Take this,' she said to Bran, handing him a shiny coin. 'A friend of mine gave me this as a present once, and I've never had an opportunity to use it. I've kept it in my bag for all this time. As you and Zach are off to cause some trouble, I think you might need it.'

Then she handed Fran and Nelson some boots. 'Seven-league boots. Good for the toughest terrain and the most magical transportation of distances up to seven leagues away.'

'Goodbye,' Fran signed to Bran.

'I'll see you in a bit,' he signed back, as he headed to the nearby forest with Zachary. 'We'll be a team again soon, I promise. The important thing is finding Mum and if we need to split up to do it, then that's what we've got to do.'

Fran nodded and gave him a quick squeeze. 'I know. Good luck.'

'Come on, come on,' said Wilma. 'Something tells me that time is of the essence.'

And with that, they left.

CHAPTER 15

Clutching his drawing paper and pencils in case he needed to write things down to be understood where they were going, Bran stood next to Zach.

'Just take a breath like you're about to swim underwater for a while, and follow me,' the Zebracorn confidently said, strolling into the woods.

Bran breathed in DEEPLY, and followed Zach's lead as he took one confident step after another, and within moments they were sliding through molecules, past stars, battling warriors, underwater with enormous sharks, whooshing past camels and Fire Lizards. Within the space of less than a minute they came to a halt and they were outside a compound made from wood and stone. Stakes were placed at intervals all around and stone spikes made up the rest of the defences.

'Whoa, looks like the Kindly Woods *do* always know where you gotta go,' Zach said.

Bran gulped. It looked like the Viking encampment from one of his favourite illustrated books, *Berserk Vikings Go Even More Berserk: Volume Two.*

There were severed heads on long sharpened poles dotted around the encampment. Zach saw how pale Bran was looking. 'They're just turnips, painted to frighten off unwanted guests.'

He continued, 'before we go any further, we're going to need that disguise you talked about.'

'I've already changed.' Bran gestured to the peasant leather jerkin and sackcloth trousers that Wilma had pulled out of her bag for him before they left. 'But *you* still need a bit of work . . .'

Bran stuffed his writing paper into his bag and soon was covering Zachary in mud and dung. Zachary was not impressed. 'This is not fun,' he muttered. 'Really not fun.'

'We *have* to cover you up,' Bran explained. He tied a cloth around Zachary's spike and smeared that with clods of mud, making it look like Zachary had a giant boil on his head. 'Because you're a Zebracorn and, as you keep telling us, there aren't very many of you guys around. So now you just look and smell like a stinky donkey with a boil on his head.'

'I only look and smell like a stinky donkey with a boil on his head because you covered me in poo!' Zachary exploded.

As he said that, the huge gates of the compound were flung open and a hundred

Bloodsword soldiers clad in metal and fur with horned helmets marched out. They were carrying a flat wooden bed, filled with hay and twigs and branches. Lying on top of that was a large man who seemed fast asleep. Only . . .

'He's not moving at all,' thought Bran. 'He must be a really deep sleeper.'

'He's not asleep, Bran,' Zach replied. 'He's dead.'

And then there was a fanfare of horns blowing and drummers drumming, women wailed and men roared in anguish. This was a flame-lit funeral procession. Huge torches were jammed into the ground around the wooden bed. As the flames illuminated the area, Bran and Zachary found themselves smack in the middle of several large guards with larger broadswords.

They all stopped and stared at Zach and Bran. They drew their swords and pointed them at the interlopers.

Bran was scared stiff.

Zach closed his eyes.

They were in the worst trouble either of them had ever been.

And then a man stepped out from within their captors. It was hard to see his face because he was so hairy he resembled a woolly  mammoth in leggings. His hair was twisted into long, dark tangled locks and he had an incredibly shaggy beard. He wore a breastplate of beaten metal with a woollen jerkin over it, and an engraved helmet with goat horns attached to it. He gestured with his hand and the solders lowered their swords.

The man turned and spoke to the crowd.

'Friends! We are here to pay our respects to Jacthawn. A truly great leader. He took me in when I arrived in this strange land, carried here by lightning.

Under his rule, we have turned our compound into a place where things work: the drains, clean water, the cold rooms for meat and fish. With my counselling, this compound is safe, our tables are well stocked with food, our fields yield bountiful crops, our children are happy, we rarely go to war and a really nice chip shop opened just 'round the corner. Now Jacthawn is dead.'

At this moment Zach looked to his left and right. There were warriors with tears streaming down their faces, mothers and children unashamedly hugging and weeping into each other's shoulders. He head-said to Bran, 'This Jacthawn was obviously loved.'

The hairy man held up a piece of parchment. 'Jacthawn's final wishes,' he said, 'were that I, Wisejest, tell three jokes, and then send him on his way into the afterlife before becoming your new chief.'

'What do you call a can opener that doesn't work? A can't opener . . .'

'What do you get from a pampered cow? Spoilt milk.'

Wisejest was crying now. And with each joke he told, the more he cried.

'You know why you never see elephants hiding up a tree? Because they're really good at it.'

People were groaning and laughing now amidst the crying. As he finished telling the final joke, Wisejest picked up a flaming torch and touched it to the hay-filled funeral bed, which went up in flames with a loud *krump!* noise. Everyone in the crowd stood, now illuminated by the fire, their faces red and glistening with tears. Wisejest placed the flaming torch back down, picked up a jug, took a swig and yelled, 'Jacthawn!'

And everyone in the camp shouted in reply, 'Jacthawn!'

The ceremony was over. Wisejest suddenly turned to Bran and Zachary. 'If you're invading us, I'm afraid it will have to wait,' he said politely. 'Our leader's funeral takes priority over any invasion by less than three people.'

Bran took in Wisejest's kind eyes and, out of habit, signed to Zachary, 'I don't think they're going to kill us.'

To Bran's surprise, Wisejest signed back. 'Of course we're not. What kind of leader would order his men to kill a child and his stinky donkey?'

Zachary muttered something under his breath which sounded a bit like 'Callin' me stinky donkey?

Least I don't look like a sheep in thigh boots!'

Bran interrupted him and signed, 'He's not actually a stinky donkey. He's more a . . . guide. Our map told us that we were needed here, that someone might be in danger – I guess that was Jacthawn. But we're not just here to pay our respects. In fact, we need your help.'

Wisejest nodded. 'We will do all we can. For a price, obviously. Please, join us for the funeral banquet.'

And he led them to the dining hall.

As they walked, Bran frowned. 'I know Wisejest from somewhere,' he head-to-head said to Zach. 'I just can't remember exactly where.'

CHAPTER 16

'**R**ight!' Fran exclaimed. 'We are going to Koto Utama, where the evil Prince lives and has captured a boatload of magical creatures and there's a strong possibility that he's also captured Mum.'

Wilma nodded. 'Thank you for that recap of our situation. Can we go now?'

Fran gave an embarrassed grin. Wilma took her by the hand and they both stepped forward.

'Now,' Wilma explained. 'Thing about seven-league boots is that they're a bit like potato crisps – once you start, you can't stop. If you don't know exactly where you're going you might overshoot.'

Which is *exactly* what happened to them.

With a whoosh and a swoosh, Wilma and Fran flew past the most amazing sights from all over the Nine Dominions. Fran was enchanted but Wilma quickly (but not quickly enough) realized that they were nowhere near Koto Utama.

They had ended up just over six leagues away, in the dominion of Wollodja.

Wollodja was the domain of the Dark Elves and their Lord Chidozie – the most mischievous Dark Elf of all. Chidozie was renowned for practical jokes on an almost cosmic level.

He told Lion there was a new rule about having short hair during the hot months and insisted he shave off his mane.

He made Elephant iron out his wrinkly skin because 'the old creased look was out of fashion, it was all about youth now'.

He had persuaded the sacred trees of Wharpen to huddle closer to the fire because a 'warm tree is a comfortable tree', and when they had caught fire, he and his entire family had used the flames to make a barbecue and steaming hot cups of exotic herbal drinks.

Chidozie did not suffer fools, unless it was he that was making the fool of them. So when his scouts spotted Wilma, Fran and Nelson tottering about in their ill-fitting boots, they were escorted to his compound immediately.

The Dark Elves shunned the idea of constant war, so they didn't need castles and fortified areas. Instead they had a massive sign painted on a nearby hillside that read IF YOU'RE REALLY STUPID, ATTACK. WE'LL MAKE SURE YOUR REMAINS GO TO THE RIGHT ADDRESS, which seemed to work just fine.

As Fran entered the compound, she started to recognize things: the atmosphere, the aromas, the colours, the clothes. These Elven women had style. They reminded Fran of . . . Mum.

She was busy gaping at the sights when Wilma gave her a dig with her elbow. 'Look lively, the boss is here.'

Chidozie, the Lord of the Dark Elves, was being carried by a giant tortoise wearing gold armour. Fran and Wilma waited for his approach. And waited. And waited.

He yelled ahead in a mischievous way, 'I know he takes his time, but it gives me a chance to get a good look at you.'

When he finally arrived, he turned his attention to Wilma first. 'I know you, you're Ephos's wife. He's a good man, Ephos. Does he know you're out and about and trying to cause trouble in my compound?'

'My trouble-causing days are behind me,' Wilma

said. 'I am here as a guide to this human girl, Your Majesty.'

'Ah, yes.' Chidozie turned his attentions to Fran. 'I think I know you too, girl. We shall dine together, and you will tell me why you are here. Let us go to the main house the quick way.'

Three large, saddled ostriches were brought out by his pointy-eared assistants. Wilma and Fran were helped up as Chidozie effortlessly jumped on, raised his arm and said, 'Last one to the compound pays for dinner!'

And he dropped his arm and raced off!

Wilma spurred her ostrich, who seemed intent on running in circles, but Fran's shot off after Chidozie. Fran held on with all her might, whispering 'You have to be brave,' under her breath repeatedly as the ostrich dashed level with Chidozie.

In the end, it was a draw.

Chidozie raised an eyebrow as he gracefully got off the giant bird. 'Well done, little human,' he said. 'A natural ostrich rider is deserving of respect.'

Fran tried to look worthy of respect as she tumbled off the ginormous bird, before being helped back up by Chidozie's silver-clad Elven attendants.

When Wilma finally made it over (even Nelson the goat, managed to make it there before her), Chidozie beckoned them to sit at a bountiful table, laid out with a glorious mixture of herbed rice and spicy vegetables and flatbreads and a variety of sauces – there were bowls of condiments and silken napkins. The Elven attendants poured out a couple of bottles of NESTA'S BEST EVER SODA, and Fran, thirsty from the ostrich race, drank the most beautiful berry-flavoured drink she had ever tasted. It was gingery and raspberry and blueberry and blackberry, and it had a fizz that bubbled in your mouth.

Wilma sipped and smiled to herself.

Chidozie intoned a prayer of welcome:

'My guests are at table, the food all prepared, .
And now friends a test before food is shared.
You must make a choice, but just so you know,
Once this meal's been tasted, the *truth* you will crow!'

Wilma and Fran looked at each other in alarm. What had he done to the food?

Chidozie smiled at them with a twinkle in his eye and explained further. 'We always prepare an introductory banquet with potions that compel our guests to tell the truth, as well as our secret mix of herbs and spices. If they are planning some kind of an attack or want to steal the silver or simply want the recipe for my ostrich con carne, it's always good to know ahead of time, so that we can deal with the problem accordingly.'

Fran, thanks to her mother's stories, had been wary of the food. Unfortunately, as they had taken their seats, Wilma had been unable to stop herself from picking at the smallest piece of flatbread and was, as Chidozie promised, ready to tell the truth.

She roared at the Elf Lord. 'Well, you are a rude little man!'

Chidozie spat out his drink in surprise.

Wilma continued, 'D'you know there's a reason no one sees you in the other dominions? You don't get invited cos no one likes you!'

A dark aura appeared around Chidozie's body as he roared back, 'How dare you, you tiny, big-mouthed shrew! I've a good mind to—'

But Wilma wouldn't let him finish. 'You miserable mongoose! We've come all this way, and all you can do is poison us and make us tell the truth! Well, you wanted it, you've got it – your compound smells of feet and so do you!'

As Fran listened to the insults coming out of Wilma's mouth and watched Chidozie's eyes darken ominously, she knew she had to do something now or they were both going to die.

She gathered her courage and spoke quickly. 'Please

don't kill us, Mr Lord Chidozie. I haven't eaten the food but I promise to tell you the truth. Your compound does smell of feet, but I've quite enjoyed being here anyway. It reminds me of my mum, who I really miss. I miss my dad too. He and my mum were both struck by lightning and left my brother Bran who really is the brave one, and me by ourselves. Mum told us all these stories and made us rice and chicken and this great sauce that smelt of curry but wasn't too spicy, it was . . .'

Chidozie stood then, in awe of the waterfall of words coming out of this small human child. But at that point he finished the sentence for her: '. . . *just right*. And there were these dumplings that, when you dipped them in the gravy and popped them in your mouth . . .'

And Fran and Chidozie completed the sentence together: '. . . they just melted beautifully – as if by magic.'

Fran gasped. 'Magic.'

Chidozie, who caught on a lot sooner (he was a very clever Elven Lord, after all), looked at her and burst into tears.

He called out, 'Wife! Daughters! Everyone!'

And suddenly from several doors came a burst of activity as Chidozie's family ran in. Chidozie looked at them all and laughed. 'Who does this girl remind you of? Tell me, quickly!'

Chidozie's wife, Chinonke, spoke clearly and with great certainty. 'Old goat, are you a fool? She looks like one of us. We must inform Oraya!'

And she clapped her hands, and a young, very fit boy appeared by her side. 'Go tell Oraya we have a new child.'

The boy whizzed off and within moments was back. 'She says we lie.'

Chinonke rolled her eyes, muttered something about how 'difficult this family was', and then looked at her husband. 'You must go to her river dwelling and show Oraya the child.'

And so Chidozie ordered the three ostriches to be saddled once more and they all climbed on.

Wilma, who was still under the influence of the truth herbs, was saying things like, 'This thing stinks,' and, 'But I bet it tastes good!'

Chidozie and Fran tried their best to ignore her as they headed for the river at speed. As they approached Oraya's encampment, he started to explain. 'Oraya has a very special relationship with animals.'

He wasn't exaggerating. As they rode along the river, Chidozie, Wilma and Fran were increasingly accompanied by aardvarks, bison, badgers, cows, crocodiles, elephants, foxes, horses, hounds, moles and sheep, who all joined them, jostling for attention, as they headed towards Oraya's dwelling.

They came to a very simple wooden dwelling where flowers erupted and seemed to intertwine with the architecture. Fran noticed that there were all types of animals, big and small, everywhere. The ones higher up on the food chain giving a wide berth to the tinier more edible ones near the bottom.

Oraya was already outside waiting for them. 'Greetings! To what do I owe this honour, Father?'

Chidozie greeted his daughter formally, 'Oraya of the Five Rivers, Guardian of All Surrounding Wildlife, Nurturer of Magical Creatures, we salute you and pray you give us welcome.'

Oraya nodded and gestured for them to follow her inside. As they lowered themselves into elegantly carved chairs at the wooden table, a lemur started pouring the drinks, and an elephant delicately offered around a fruit tray that was balanced on its trunk.

Fran's mind was a mush at this point, not least because Oraya was staring at her intently. 'So who are you and why are you here?' she asked slowly.

Fran opened her mouth to speak but before she could begin her story, Chidozie interrupted. 'Seven-league boots they used to get here! As if trying to get the beauty of our dominion out of the way!'

'Yes, Father,' Oraya said. 'But as I was asking the girl . . .'

Fran opened her mouth again to speak, when a deep booming voice suddenly appeared as if from the skies – which is actually where the creature who owned it hovered above them.

'I'll bet it's to do with the wedding.'

Fran looked up and saw a large dragon flapping its

wings overhead. 'Any sheep left, Oraya? I'm starving.'

'The food chain can be difficult for some,' Oraya explained to her guests. 'Dragons are fiercely carnivorous beings, no matter how nice they are.'

She raised her head to the sky at the waiting dragon. 'Can't you at least *try* the fruit basket?'

'Look at the size of me, do I look like I want the fruit basket?'

'You said you'd try!' said Oraya, sounding exasperated. 'You said you'd give the whole "Let's not eat each other" plan a go – it's why I let you stay here!'

'Fine,' muttered the dragon. 'Sling me the meatiest-looking fruit, quick.'

Oraya tossed the dragon a mango and turned back to Fran and Wilma. 'Now, if the interruptions are over, please, continue with why you are here in the Nine Dominions.'

'We come seeking your help,' Wilma explained. 'This girl's mother is missing.' She looked from Oraya to Fran and back again. 'And,' she said slowly, 'I believe that you two might be related.'

Fran dropped an orange in shock. A mongoose ran across and grabbed it, said, 'Waste not, want not!' and scurried back to where it came from.

'Yes,' whispered Chidozie. 'I knew I wasn't imagining it.'

Oraya looked at Fran. Fran looked at Oraya.

'She can't be . . .' Oraya whispered. 'And yet, they are so alike.'

'I can't be who?' demanded Fran, who was freaking out a little.

Oraya said quietly, 'Are you Effiya's child?'

Fran nodded.

'Then your mother is my sister.'

Chidozie was sobbing now.

'But – but that doesn't make any sense,' said Fran, bewildered. 'My mother lived in Ruthvale with Ken the handyman. Not the Nine Dominions!'

'No,' said Oraya, her voice gathering in strength. 'Your mother was the Elven princess, betrothed to Prince Roger. The date for the wedding was set and she journeyed to the palace. Soon after, we started getting the weirdest letters, all about fishing. Effiya hates fish. I never liked that prince. I like him even less now that it's clear he's been lying to us. Your mother must've escaped and travelled to where you're from. The Ruthvale dominion, did you say?'

'Rumour has it that Prince Roger has taken a new bride,' said the dragon from above. 'A beautiful princess who arrived in a flash of lightning and has been half asleep ever since. They call her the Dreaming Princess.'

Wilma, Chidozie, Oraya and Fran all stared at each other.

'My mother,' said Fran at last, 'is the Dreaming Princess.'

She could not stop watching her auntie: Oraya *had* to be family, she had the same long, thick black hair, same eyes, same skin, same shape – *everything*.

Apart from the slightly odd preoccupation with animals (like Dr Dolittle in a dress, Fran thought), Oraya was a carbon copy of her mum. Chidozie grinned a happy, wolf-like grin and said, 'I have a granddaughter!'

'Actually,' Fran said. 'There's two of us. My twin

brother Bran is travelling to the castle now.'

And with that, Chidozie leapt in the air and howled with joy. 'Grandchildren!' he yelled.

Everything around on four legs, or three, or six, or eight – joined in with him in celebration: HOWWWWWWWWWWWWWWWWWWW WWWWWWWWWWLLLLLLLLLLLL!

CHAPTER

Time seemed to work differently at the Bloodsword compound in Zaharda. A minute passed like an hour. Once Bran got used to it, he liked having all the extra time in this strange new world.

Bran and Zachary spent it getting to know Wisejest. He was a superb chief and had immediately assigned one of his best commanders, Leyna, to be Bran's interpreter. He was always going to fix the watermill at the river or taste Mrs Emerson's pies (part of his job as chieftain was to decide on the two pies to be eaten at meal times).

Wisejest didn't like random fighting, particularly if it was over a pie. He thought everything should be solved with common sense and discussion, but still made sure that everyone took part in battle training (they were Bloodswords after all).

Bran found himself with older boys and girls who already knew their way around a sword. They taught him how to thrust, parry and go in for the kill. He didn't like this last bit, but Wisejest told him there wasn't any point learning how to fight with a sword if you weren't going to jab the pointy bit into your opponent at some point.

Zach didn't like it either. One afternoon as they watched Bran fight, he said to Wisejest, 'He's forty-eight seasons old, too young to know the ways of war.'

Wisejest shook his head. He was a great leader who didn't mind answering to a still-stinky donkey. 'We would never use violence unless we had to. We train every man, woman and child so that they know how to hide, run, send messages, swim, climb, and then drop large rocks on the enemy. Swordplay is a last resort but a necessary one, especially since the magic started fading.'

Just then, a great cheer went up from a circle of young men as Bran flipped one of them over and held the pointy end of his wooden sword to his opponent's neck. Bran turned to Zach and Wisejest, and signed, 'That was amazing! It's like I've been fighting like this all my li—'

The reason the word 'life' wasn't finished was because his opponent jumped up and whacked him on the back of his head with the side of his sword.

'Hey!' cried Zach. 'That's not fair!'

Wisejest replied, 'In a real battle, there is no fair.'

Later at dinner, Bran was guest of honour at Wisejest's dining table. He sat to the new chieftain's left, whilst Zach was given pride of place outside the tent (he was still very stinky).

'I have enjoyed getting to know you and your stinky donkey,' Wisejest signed to Bran as they finished their stew. 'Why don't you tell me a bit more about how I can help you?'

Bran spread out the Impossible Map. 'It took us

here for a reason,' he explained. 'But I think now we need to go to Koto Utama.'

They all looked at the dot on the map that hovered over the city of Koto Utama. It was glowing so brightly with danger that it was smoking.

'My sister's there!' Bran signed. 'And we think my mum might be too. I think the map knows what we want and is sending us there. Please will you help us?'

'I'd like to help,' Wisejest replied thoughtfully. 'But my duties are to the compound. Speaking of, now that the meal is over. . .'

With that, he jumped on the stage and did a tight ten-minute comedy set, reducing the room to laughter. He was just about to start his encore when a ragged soldier wearing a royal uniform ran into the room.

Two Bloodswords drew their weapons, but Wisejest held up a hand.

The herald spoke. 'O great leader, forgive me for interrupting your jokes. I have a letter for you from Handsome Prince Roger of Koto Utama.'

'Please read it, will you?' said Wisejest.

The soldier cleared his throat and said, 'The soon-to-be King of Koto Utama commands you and your best men to act as security for the royal wedding. Three boxes of gold will be made available to you after the wedding. Yours, Prince Roger, soon to be King of Koto Utama, etc. etc.'

Wisejest stood up. 'Men, women, boys, girls, it appears we have been offered employment.'

A great cheer went up in the dining hall.

'Handsome Prince Roger would have us travel to Koto Utama and provide protection for him and his bride on their wedding day.'

Another big cheer went up.

'And,' said Wisejest, 'three boxes full of gold will be given to us after the ceremony.'

The Bloodswords cheered again. But Wisejest paused and slowly looked around the room as he continued. 'But there's something wrong with this offer. Can anyone tell me what it is?'

The patient way he asked the question reminded Bran very much of someone.

Warriors sat with furrowed brows, trying to work out what might be wrong with this deal. Wisejest asked again, 'Anyone?'

A tousle-headed child stood up at the back of the room. He yelled, 'We get paid upfront normally.'

There were lots of 'Oh'- and 'Ah'- and 'Yes'- and 'Of course'-type comments going around the room. Wisejest threw a coin at the child, who caught it easily and stuffed it in his pocket gratefully.

'Yes. We get paid upfront always. The Prince knows that. Which makes me think there is something fishy about this deal. Which reminds me . . . What do you call a fish with no eye? Fsh. Why are fish so easy to weigh? They have their own scales. What did the shark say after eating a clown fish? That tasted funny to me.'

The herald laughed despite himself, and persisted. 'Prince Roger was really quite insistent . . .'

Wisejest shook his head. 'No money, no Bloodswords.'

Zach popped his head into the hall at this point

and turned to Wisejest. 'We need to go to the castle too, to find Bran's sister and hopefully his mom. Can't we go there together?'

Wisejest hesitated. 'We march for gold upfront. That's how it's always been.'

'Wait a sec,' signed Bran. He reached into the pocket of his jerkin. 'A friend of mine gave *me* a present. Would this help pay for you to help us?' He produced a glowing coin. It illuminated the entire room.

'That is a luck penny,' Wisejest gasped in awe. 'More valuable than gold, silver and diamonds. More than enough to pay for us to travel to Koto Utama.'

Wisejest looked around at his people. 'Everybody get ready. We're marching double-time to the castle.'

CHAPTER 18

Wilma looked down at their seven-league boots.

'It's a shame these aren't more accurate at transporting. Koto Utama is at least nine leagues away. If we don't hit it exactly, we'll never get there in time for the wedding.'

Oraya looked at them both. 'I have a dragon. They can fly very quickly, though I'm not sure he could support all of us . . .'

'Maybe if I had some decent protein in me, like a sheep, say, or one of those cows, I could carry more,' the dragon interjected.

Fran looked distressed. 'We have to get there

as soon as we can!' she insisted.

'What we need is some kind of carriage on tracks that sort of propels you to where you wanna go – but really quickly,' Wilma added thoughtfully.

Fran resisted the urge to yell 'THAT'S A TRAIN!' at the top of her lungs. This was hopeless.

Chidozie had an idea. 'Can't you get in touch with your husband?' he asked Wilma. 'He is known for his questing, and surely rescuing my daughter from the castle is a quest.'

Oraya and Fran looked at Wilma expectantly.

Wilma grinned. 'Well, If I'm going to convince Ephos to do anything for me, I'll need a large pot of tea and a bucket full of shame and grief.'

In the snowy mountains of Unsayth, a dreadlocked wizard and his twelve dwarf companions dug their way through the drifts of snow and complained bitterly about the cold. The wizard tried to raise their spirits.

'C'mon, everyone,' he said cheerfully. 'Let us not allow the cold to defeat us.'

A dwarf, whose name was Steve, and who seemed to be operating as some kind of large packhorse for everybody else, snorted.

'Are you telling us to cheer up, wizard? Put on a brave face? Whistle a happy tune? I'm not going to do that. I've been on donkey duty since we started this stupid trip. The minute I see this evil black hole that's supposed to destroy our world and everything in it, I'm chucking all this rubbish in there.'

Another dwarf, called Idris, pushed through the snow, shoulder-deep and shivering.

'C'mon, don't be like that. We're nearly there. We have triumphed over Mud Monsters, Spirits of the Sphere, Fire Lizards and the worst catering in the Nine Dominions.'

Gary, a third dwarf in a chef's hat, practically swam through a snowdrift to be a part of this argument.

'Oi!' he said. 'Insulting my food, are you? If it wasn't for my dumplings and rice and hot wings and barbecue duck, we would have all passed away from hunger months ago.'

Steve shook his head. 'That's a point. I'm carrying a ruddy great barbecue and nobody else has offered to help.'

The dreadlocked wizard watched wearily as the dwarves argued amongst themselves and started taking the odd jab at each other. It was time for him to play referee.

'All right, all right. We'll make camp here,' he said. 'We'll have tea and finger sandwiches, and there might be some ham and some crusty bread left.'

Gary muttered under his breath.

'And when we're all done, pick up after yourselves. I'm not your maid.'

And a huge repast suddenly appeared before them, and there were, indeed, finger sandwiches, slices of ham, chicken, mutton, big slabs of crunchy bread, salty butter and flagons of ale, and everyone tore into the food as if they hadn't eaten for months (even though at lunchtime they had devoured whole roast chickens, baked potatoes, cabbages, cauliflowers, spicy hot yellow rice, and apple pie and custard).

Ephos the wizard (for it was he) was about to sip from a large mug of tea when he almost dropped it into his lap. Looking out at him from the milky tea was Wilma's face.

'I thought you weren't talking to me?'

Wilma gave him a tight smile and said, 'Well, you are wrong. I need your help. I'm on a quest of my own.'

Ephos snaffled the last two finger sandwiches. 'But I thought our marriage was over. You said some mean things.'

'Only because you made me angry,' Wilma replied. 'You'd just got home. I was so happy to see you. The house has been so empty since our son left. Then you tell me that you've been booked for another adventure the next week. It just feels like you don't want to be with me.'

Ephos mumbled into his cup of tea. 'Of course I want to be with you. I love you.'

There was a cheer from behind Wilma. Ephos peered into the teacup. 'Who's that?'

Wilma replied, 'That's Fran, the human child we need to help. Her brother's gone to recruit the Bloodswords from Zaharda, and we're all meeting at the castle in time to rescue their mum.'

Ephos shook his head.

'This is the quest you're on?'

Wilma nodded.

'Yes, but we'll never get there in time if you don't help.'

Ephos considered for a moment.

'I have the lightning spear with me. I can transport you to Koto Utama in the blink of an eye. Let me just let the team know I have to leave them for a moment.'

He stood up, looked at the dwarves, who were all full of sandwiches, and chicken legs, and crunchy bread, and said, 'We'll spend the night here, make fires, put up the tents, stay warm. Make sure you set a watch on the hour, every hour. Clear up the mess and pack everything away. I'll be back shortly.'

He picked up his bag, swirled his cape, banged his staff four times on the ground, and disappeared. Steve looked at the rest of his fellow travellers and saw that they were all already asleep.

'Typical. I s'pose muggins here has got to do all the cleaning. Again.' And he began the arduous task of cleaning up everybody else's mess.

In the blink of a tarantula's eye, Ephos was standing with Wilma, Fran and Nelson outside Oraya's home. She had set off on the dragon already.

The wizard asked them to hold hands and face in the direction of Koto Utama. He waved his staff around seven times, then banged it hard on the ground seven times. Thunderclouds appeared and big fat blobs of rain began to fall.

And then several majestic lightning hooks appeared. Each bolt seemed to have a personality of its own. There was a golden one, a silver one and an emerald one, which struck time and time again before a circle had been burned around Fran and the others. Ephos rammed his staff into the ground and the lightning bolts darted from the sky with a KRAKA-THOOOM! – and they vanished.

There was a flurry of smoke and wind and rain and sparks, and when it all cleared, Ephos nodded his head and said,

'My work is done.'

He spun around three times and, in a heartbeat, was back on the snowy mountain helping Steve clear up.

'Sorry I had to nip off.'

Steve looked at him with a beady eye.

'Yeah, thanks for coming back, now that I've almost finished. Typical wizard, always disappears when the hard work happens.'

Ephos shook his head and began collecting what was left of the plates and cutlery.

CHAPTER 19

T here were more people than usual on the road to the city, some in carriages that had seen better days, but most on foot. It didn't take much detective work to figure out that they were all heading towards Prince Roger's castle for the royal wedding which was taking place later that afternoon.

The prince was finally marrying and, according to the decree his father King Nelson (now deceased) had written, this marriage meant that Prince Roger would now become *King* Roger of the Nine Dominions.

There was a lot of talk about how things were to be put right in the city and surrounding areas once the prince was happy. Less talk about why that would be so.

They overheard all sorts of conversations on their way to the castle.

'Aw, yes, he hasn't been happy for a while, has he?'

'Good-looking boy like him, what's he got to be miserable about?'

'She was away on her toes, wasn't she?'

'Yes, and he never recovered. I dunno why. She's beautiful, but she's not *that* beautiful.'

'Well, what are you calling beautiful? Your missus is a handsome woman by any standards, but compared to the princess, she looks like a moose.'

'Well, your missus looks like a warthog.'

The two men began an outrageous slapping fight. No blows seemed to be landing. As Fran and Wilma and Nelson (the goat, not the old king) headed past them and on towards the city, they could hear the tail end of the argument disappearing into the distance.

'Moose!'

'Warthog!'

'Trout face!'

'Duck's bum!'

And then a few more faint slaps before the sounds of the altercation faded completely.

'Look!' breathed Fran. 'That must be the castle!'

'Yes,' Wilma sighed. 'What a wonderful wedding venue it makes.'

The castle dominated the horizon. The exterior was large and menacing, with ostentatious brickwork and castellated roof towers. There was a moat and sharpened metal points dotted around the walls to prevent intruders. There were cavities near the tops of each wall through which a medium-sized snapping turtle could be shoved and dispense severe nips to any attacker's nose.

'What do we do now?' said Fran.

'We need to get into the castle,' said Wilma. In the distance, she could see what looked like of an entire legion of horned warriors marching in the direction of the well-fortified castle. 'Which is impossible.'

Just then, Fran saw a wizard clambering up some kind of platform near the castle gates.

The wizard addressed the gathered throng:

'Gathered throng, my name is Babadock –

There is a singing contest that you have to rock.
Get up here and sing your heart out,
Let the whole world know what you are all about,
Sing about birds and sing about bees,
Sing about the berries in the hawthorn trees,
And whoever sings the best will be watered and fed,
And they'll win a pot of gold when the Prince gets
wed.'

Everyone clapped at this impromptu spot of rhymed speech. Babadock bowed and scraped to the horde of people who were lined up, desperate for the chance to be at the wedding.

'It's a competition,' Fran explained to Wilma. 'Whoever sings the best gets to perform at the wedding!'

A tall, thin man played a flute and sang in the gaps, which did not go down as well as he thought it might, owing to the fact that he couldn't really sing. Or play the flute.

Then three people, two men and a woman got up and sang in three-part harmony, but weren't quite as

214

in tune as they thought. The crowd were quite cruel.

'But why can't we throw tomatoes at them? They're terrible!'

'Because the tomatoes might hurt them.'

'Yeah, well their singing's hurting me!'

'You can throw *one* tomato.'

'*Thank* you!'

Shortly after this, a healer was called to attend to the tenor singer with the large tomato-shaped bruise smack dab in the middle of his forehead.

Fran knew that the only way she was going to get into the castle was if she sang. But the only person she was brave enough to sing for was Mum.

She stood there nervously. She knew what she had to do. She would take part in the contest and she would win it.

Fran turned to Wilma. 'I'm going to sing one of the songs from my mum's book. Now that I think about it, she must have been writing about my auntie.'

And without looking back, Fran marched up to the competition platform.

The Ballad of Oraya
and the Pixie

The maiden in the tower with the locks of jet-black
    hair
And skin as dark as ebony, so dark yet oh so fair,
Was captured by a pixie – a creature bent and old,
Who locked her up with a spinning wheel and said
    'You will spin gold!'

So she worked and toiled with sweat and strain and
    produced bags of gold,
She did it once, she did it again – and the pixie was so
    bold,
He said, 'If you continue to spin like this – I'll make
    you be my wife!'
The maiden with the locks so black was full of dread
    and strife.

She did not wish to marry the man who forced her to
spin gold,
His features were sharp and wrinkled so, and he was
terribly, terribly old,
His hands and fingers were strong like flint, his nails
as sharp as a knife,
Marrying him was oh so wrong – she did not want to
be his wife.

So while she spun the threads of gold, she planned a
plan so well:
She had no handsome prince to come and rescue her
from this hell,
So she thought about what she might do, to escape
this evil tower,
Then one fine morning, before he arrived, came such a
fateful hour!

She made the pixie a suit of gold from her finest
golden thread,
He came, and saw, and pulled the shirt proudly over
his head,
He put the jacket on, and was instantly proud of the
perfect fit,
He zipped into his trousers and suddenly something
bit!

Within the thread she'd sewn red ants that bit him
through the cloth,
And as they bit, he danced around and yelled with
pain and wrath,
He danced so hard in the golden suit, his voice grew
rough and hoarse,
They bit him everywhere they could – they bit with
power and force.

And he wriggled and jiggled and twirled and whirled

And it seemed he might not stop

And he whirled so much and he whirled so fast

He resembled a spinning top . . .

And he spun off into the distance

And he yelped and screamed with pain

And everyone knew the pixie had earned just desserts

And he was never seen again . . .

Oh, he was never seen again!

The End

Fran's voice was clear and tuneful. As she sang, the crowd fell silent in admiration and, at least temporarily, stopped throwing tomatoes.

The Eighteenth Chief Imperial Wizard and, for today, wedding entertainment judge, was swept up in the emotion of it – tears were in his eyes at the maiden's predicament in the early parts of the song, and then he broke out cheering at the bitey-ants part.

When she finished, he burst into applause.

'That's a great song. It felt *real* and *painful*. You have to sing at the royal wedding later today.'

Fran did a little dance and looked around for Wilma. They were in!

But her celebration was soon interrupted by the buzzing of fast-approaching Murder Fairies who had surrounded a pocket-sized Viking who had somehow managed to sneak up to the castle's exterior.

Fran recognized him straight away. It was Bran, and, judging by his pointy helmet, it looked like he had been serving as some sort of advance scout for the Bloodswords.

'Aha!' squeaked Zzzt, the leader of the Murder Fairies. 'Not so brave without your shovels, are you?'

'What do you want?' cried Fran, trying to swat away the fierce little winged creatures.

'You can find out at the castle,' Zzzt said. 'Now get moving.'

'I WON'T cried Fran, but the Murder Fairies swept her towards the castle with such force, her feet didn't touch the ground. They were small, but they were very, very, strong.

Within moments, both Bran and Fran were at the castle gates, which flew open to allow them inside, the Murder Fairies' triumphant buzzing growing louder and louder as the fortified gates slammed shut behind them. They were in the courtyard now, surrounded by armed soldiers, all levelling weapons at them, and yet more Murder Fairies.

Bran gulped. Then he signed to Fran, 'Well, this is where we wanted to end up, isn't it?'

And then there were two thumps and both Bran and Fran fell to the ground, unconscious.

CHAPTER 20

Koto Utama Castle was a labyrinthine building – a place built to keep things hidden, with secrets behind closed doors and within its lower depths. There were basement chambers and cells and upper attics, work rooms, bedrooms, dens, drawing rooms, laboratories, snugs, foyers, mezzanines, kitchens, and several cat flaps.

The princess was awake and, once again, confused. She had been like this ever since she arrived at this castle. The people here were pleasant, the food tasted good, her husband-to-be seemed like a nice person. Husband-to-be? But she *had a husband, didn't she*? Her memories whizzed around in her head for a moment.

She saw books, children yelling, herself telling stories, and a kind-faced man holding a screwdriver in one hand and a teacake in the other.

She shook her head, and the memories vanished promptly. Today she was getting ready for the big wedding. She sat up and waited for Babadock, who seemed to be more or less nice. She wondered if there was something not quite right about where she was. She certainly recognized aspects of the room where she slept, the windows, walls and carpets looked *familiar.*

She shook her head again and forced herself to think through what was about to happen. Babadock would escort her to the ceremony and . . . but just then she was distracted by a beautiful voice singing about a maiden in a tower and insects biting a pixie, which made her smile and cry all at the same time.

She knew this voice. Or at least she thought she did.

It was a sweet, tuneful sound – a cross between Little Mix and Whitney Houston. A heartfelt sound that pierced the princess's very soul.

Babadock entered her bedroom.

'Princess, the time has come for your wedding.'

'Who was that singing earlier?' she asked. 'I would love to meet her.'

'There's no time, I'm afraid,' said Babadock. He had a strict itinerary and it was more than his life was worth (literally) to deviate from it.

'Oh please,' said the princess, with tears in her eyes. 'Her voice is so pure and sweet.'

Babadock hesitated, and then, because he was nice, he nodded. A small diversion couldn't hurt.

'Thank you,' the princess said as he led the way out.

She followed Babadock to the lower depths of the castle where the jail cells lay. He called out ahead, 'Start singing, songbird, the princess is here to see you.'

And as the cells grew closer, the singing became louder. The voice was at the peak of the song, where a key change occurs and the singer tells us, that she will, indeed, *always love us*, when it came to a halt as

225

the princess rounded the corner.

There was a silence. The princess stared and stared. All of those pieces started whirling around in her brain again. *Books, children yelling, herself telling stories, hot chocolate and marshmallows . . .*

The princess spoke. 'You have a beautiful voice. But then you always did, Fran.'

Then she looked at Bran, and signed, 'Bran, why are you dressed like a Viking? I've missed you both so much.'

Babadock instantly, terribly, realized what had happened. Hearing her daughter's singing must've brought the princess's memories back. He interrupted the reunion and grabbed her by the arm. 'Come on, Princess, we need to go NOW.'

He gestured at the two soldiers behind him to bring Bran and Fran along. Then he whispered to the now alert Princess, 'I know your magic is powerful but if you want to keep your twins safe, you better cooperate.'

Effiya fought and squirmed. 'Leave my children

alone! They've done nothing wrong.'

Babadock stopped, took out his wand, and placed a freezing spell on all of them. It wouldn't do for Handsome Prince Roger's adoring public to be distracted by the bride and her offspring trying to escape.

The frozen princess and her children arrived at the castle courtyard just in time to see Prince Roger make his sensational entrance, driving a carriage drawn by a dozen white horses. He performed a magnificent circuit of the royal courtyard, receiving cheers and cries of joy from his admiring populace along the way. When he reached the podium, he stood in the perfect position for the sun to catch the dimple in his chin, the ruggedness of his cheekbones and the glory of his eyes.

'My gentle people. Know that this is the happiest day of my life. I am overjoyed to introduce you all, finally, to the woman who I intend to be my wife. Her beauty and, indeed, her magic is renowned throughout the Nine Dominions.'

There were tumultuous cheers from the crowd and a . . . rumble. A rumble and the flapping of enormous wings. A rumble, the flapping of enormous wings, and the sound of a large group of men singing a marching song. Sensing something was about to go very wrong, Prince Roger gestured to Babadock that the ceremony should begin *now*. And then—

But I suppose you're wondering what happened to a certain Zebracorn disguised as a stinky donkey?

CHAPTER 21

Bran and Zachary had volunteered to sprint ahead and see just what was happening at the castle before the rest of the Bloodswords arrived. But while Bran was spotted and captured, Zachary – who the Murder Fairies assumed was merely a stinky donkey with a boil on his head – was ignored. He was left to roam the castle, pretty much as he pleased.

First of all, the Zebracorn had a good nosey around. He trotted around the boundaries of the castle and noted the big, fortified metal gates at the front. He also noticed something else. There was a basement stables at the far north-east of the castle.

Then he took a break, munching the straggly

grass that grew near the stables, and thinking things through.

'Yeah, that's right. I'm the one. I gotta rescue everybody. Me, on my own. It's just not fair. Everybody I know is in danger except for the goat who don't do nothing but eat and fire pellets from his rear end. How am I supposed to rescue Fran, Bran and whoever else I've got to rescue? It ain't right.'

'Do you always talk to yourself? I'm trying to get some rest.'

Zachary whipped round. The voice seemed to be coming from the stable.

'Who is that?' Zachary said suspiciously.

The voice from the cell said, 'My name is Zuleka. My friends used to call me Zu. Have you got any food out there?'

Zachary replied, 'Just some manky old grass.'

Zu sighed. 'I'm bored of grass. You see, we Zebracorns have very finely attuned tastebuds.'

Zachary gasped. 'A Zebracorn? You're a Zebracorn?'

The voice from the cell didn't say anything; there was a small sniff. Zachary continued, 'It's just that . . . I'm a Zebracorn too! They took all my friends away. It's just me now. Well, I say just me. Are you really a Zebracorn?'

The voice from the cell said, 'Yes,' very quietly. Zachary ran around the clearing next to the cells fourteen times. He was full of excitement. He had found another Zebracorn!

'I can't believe it, I can't believe it, I can't believe it. There's another Zebracorn. Z-E-B-R-A-C-O-R-N. Zebracorn! Oh my gosh! That means we can be friends and hang out.'

The voice laughed. 'You should be so lucky. I can smell you from here – you stink. Shame, because if we pair up, then we could access our powers.'

Zachary stopped short. 'What powers?'

Zuleka replied, 'Let me put it this way. I wouldn't have to stay in here for much longer, and you could rescue anyone you needed to.'

'Wait here!' cried Zachary.

Then he trotted until he found a drinking trough for horses. It was huge, and held gallons of fresh, clean water. There was no one around so he took a running jump and said to himself, 'Up, up and awaaaay!'

He landed with a splash and rolled around in the trough, scraping the dung off his skin and face and legs until he was clean, coat spotty and horn gleaming. Zachary stood up in the trough, jumped out, and then trotted back, carefully hiding himself from any passing soldiers.

When he got back to the cell he yelled out, 'Yow, Zuleka! Hullooooo!'

And as he yelled, the voice inside the cell said, 'Keep it down! Now walk around to the main door.'

He did as he was asked and the next thing he knew, there was a CLUMP! A THUMP! And a WHAM! After which there appeared huge dents in the thick metal doors, but something kept whamming and bamming and thumping and c-c-c-crumping until eventually the entire door flew off and slid across the courtyard!

Zachary held his breath. Standing in front of him

was the most beautiful Zebracorn he had ever seen.

'C'mon, there's going to be a wedding and we need to stop that foolishness right now!' she said.

'Not on your own,' Wilma said. (Turns out the Murder Fairies had also overlooked the old lady with the goat.) 'Bran and Fran have got us this far, but I think we're going to need some reinforcements.'

And with that, a giant dragon's shadow appeared overhead and a voice boomed from above.

'Before we go any further, has *anyone* thought about catering? I could eat a water buffalo with a big pile of butter beans . . .'

CHAPTER 22

The wedding ceremony had begun.

But the atmosphere wasn't like that of a normal wedding. Or even a normal royal wedding. Despite the general nastiness of Prince Roger, the crowds had still been excited at first, but after a bound princess and two frozen looking kids had been dragged onto the platform, it hardly felt like the time for cheering or flag-waving. The crowd now stood as if they'd had advance warning of a train crash and wanted to secure a good place from which to watch.

The prince himself strode up and down imperiously whilst waiting for proceedings to begin. He could feel the magic emanating from his bride-to-be. Bran and

Fran glared at him – but they were all still held by a magical freezing spell Babadock had put on them.

And next to them all was Effiya. She too was frozen solid by Babadock's spell – with arms and leg shackled for good measure. As the loud, festive music played from all around, the important-looking wedding officiator, wearing a rather too tall pointed hat, started the ceremony from his bejewelled and illuminated book.

Prince Roger smiled. It was all coming together. Once he was married, he would become King Roger, unite the Nine Dominions and assemble an army of such force there would be no stopping him. And once Babadock zapped Effiya of her magic and transferred it to him, he would be King Roger the Unstoppable. He would be the most powerful being in all the land.

Babadock, for his part, started to operate the controls of the magic transformation device when a large dragon-shaped shadow appeared over everyone's heads and a single burst of flame lit up the sky.

'What is this interruption?' called Prince Roger.

And that's when the Princess's sister, Oraya, who

had arrived riding on the back of her dragon, yelled, 'To me, *now*!'

Suddenly the sky was filled with birds of all kinds: buzzards, falcons, buzzhawks, kestrels, black kites, condors, enormous golden eagles and osprey.

The ground surged, lurched and undulated with a moving carpet of squirrels, beavers, black rats, hamsters, chinchillas. And German Shepherds, Siberian huskies, golden retrievers, bull terriers, Dobermanns, Rottweilers, Great Danes, Jack Russells and Dalmatians all bounded into the courtyard.

The animals snarled and shrieked as they surrounded the podium.

Wisejest pushed his way through the crowd. 'Prince Roger,' he called. 'You sent for us and we have now arrived.'

Prince Roger's gorgeous eyes darted uneasily around the Bloodswords. 'Where is Jacthawn?'

'Jacthawn died. *I* am the Bloodswords' leader now,' Wisejest explained.

'All right, all right,' snapped Prince Roger. 'Seize

these interlopers and their dogs and their, um, birds. And shoot down that dragon!'

Wisejest folded his arms. 'We do not work unless we're paid upfront.'

Prince Roger shook his head frantically. 'But I can't pay you until after the ceremony!'

He pointed to the princess and lowered his voice. 'Between you and me, soon as I get the princess's magic, I'll be able to create as many bags of gold for you as you want.'

Wisejest shrugged. 'Sounds a bit shady to me. No deal.' And he signalled to Oraya, who still hovered overhead aboard the dragon. 'I believe that's your cue?'

Oraya made a simple gesture, and immediately a further kit and caboodle of beasts pounced onto the wedding platform and attacked Prince Roger. Dogs bit, rats nibbled, eagles clawed, guinea pigs gnawed. The prince's few guards, who already felt they were underpaid and under-appreciated, scarpered.

Prince Roger turned to his wizard and shrieked, 'Babadock, activate the machine so I can steal her magic! NOW!'

Babadock looked around at the chaos and said,
'We can't do anything until you're legally married,
Your Highness. That's what makes it official . . . and
not superficial.' He stopped himself before he spat out
another thirty-two bars of rhyming slang.

Suddenly Wilma's voice rang out from the crowd.
'Babadock?! So THIS is where you are?'

'Mum?' replied Babadock, suddenly sounding less
like a Chief Imperial Wizard and more like a sulky
teenager in the deepest of trouble.

'You leave home, your room's a rubbish tip, you
don't write or even send a homing pigeon; I know I
didn't raise you like this! Your father's always out of
the house on his quests, and it turns out you're here
in the big city causing trouble, about to steal magic
from this poor princess! I don't know what to think,
Babadock. Is this really what you want out of life?'

Babadock dropped his head in shame as he stepped
away from the magical transformation machine. His
mother was right. Court Wizard to an evil prince was

not the career path he would have chosen, given the chance. He thought he might be a poet or a musician, or maybe both?

'You're right,' he said miserably. 'I'm sorry, Mum. I've done some really bad things just because the prince told me to. I used lightning magic to kidnap the princess – only I kidnapped her husband by mistake and had to wipe his memory. And then I finally kidnapped the princess and wiped *her* memory, all so she could marry the prince and he could get rich and conquer the Nine Dominions. I knew it was a terrible thing to do . . .'

'STOP THIS SILLY CHATTER!' Prince Roger pulled out clumps of his hair and batted away various vermin. 'THIS IS NOT WHAT I PLANNED.'

He pushed Babadock out of the way so hard he fell off the podium.

KA-THUMP!

Babadock was momentarily out cold and as a result, the spell he had cast to keep Bran and Fran shackled wore off.

Wilma ran towards her son to make sure he hadn't broken anything.

Bran and Fran ran towards Mum to set her free.

'Mum!' Fran cried.

'Mum!' signed Bran.

'Kids!' yelled the princess. 'Ken!'

Wisejest looked at the princess. All the glamours and confusion caused by Babadock's memory-wiping fell away.

'Effiya,' he whispered, as his memories came flooding back.

'Dad!!' Fran exclaimed as Bran's eyebrows lifted in disbelief.

But this was no time for a family reunion. The remaining castle guards rallied, the Murder Fairies buzzed angrily, and the battle raged between them, the Bloodswords, and various weasels, bull frogs, anacondas and a particularly aggressive ferret, who kept yelling to anyone who would listen, 'JUS' TRY TO LAND ONE PUNCH 'PON ME – TRY! I WI' BOX YU INTO THE MIGGLE OF NEX' WEEK!'

The prince cowered behind his throne and urged the Murder Fairies to 'DECIMATE! ANNIHILATE! Oh come on, slap them really hard!'

In the middle of the chaos, Bran caught Wilma's eye and nodded towards the temporarily abandoned magical transfer machine.

Then two enormous Zebracorns rounded the corner. They glowed yellow, purple, silver, green and black. Beams flew from their horns, knocking the castle guards off their feet and bringing down the Murder Fairies from the sky.

Effiya looked at her family. Her brave, reunited family.

'Shall we wind this up?'

She turned to Bran and held out a hand. Then Ken stretched out one to Fran. And, just like that, the Harrison family all held hands in a circle.

Everything stopped. Everyone was frozen. No one moved.

Fran gently released her hands and started to tentatively sign, 'Is this magic?'

Effiya smiled. 'It's the best kind of magic. Prince
Roger didn't realize that when a Dark Elven princess
makes a family, their magic quadruples. We are four
times more powerful together than when we are on
our own.'

Zachary and Zuleka trotted over. 'Same thing with
us. We're bigger, stronger, more powerful and better
together.'

A howl made them all turn. With a scream of rage, the prince sprinted over to the transformation machine.

'I'll do this myself,' he said determinedly through gritted teeth.

The Harrison family watched as he frantically began turning knobs and winding wheels.

'No,' cried Babadock, who had come to and was being fussed over by Wilma, who was once again by his side. 'It won't work! You don't know how to operate it! Besides,' he said, looking at his mum, 'I'm beginning to think it's not a great idea for someone like you to have all that power anyway.'

'That's where you're wrong!' Prince Roger yelled at the top of his voice. The cords stood out on his neck. His face contorted. He bared his teeth. He no longer looked handsome, but more like an angry, spoilt child.

'I make the rules, not you. I decide because I am the prince. I've waited all this time. The magic is mine. And soon, I will be king of EVERYTHING.'

The barrel of the transformation machine was

pointed at the Harrison family and began to glow orange, yellow, purple. Prince Roger cried out triumphantly, 'Yes! Yes! Yes! Yes! Yes! It's working! And I shall have four times as much magic.'

He seized the wheel and began to turn it.

'No!' cried Babadock, running towards the prince.

Unfortunately, just as the prince was about to turn the wheel which would trigger the transformation, a THOUSAND red bitey ants crawled up his right trouser leg.

The ants nibbled his legs and he began to jerk and move. His legs wiggled and jiggled, his arms flapped, his head rocked from side to side and, because he was trying to shake ants out of his pants, his bottom wobbled at an alarming rate. He yelled, 'I will get my revenge!'

He lunged for the wheel and spun it with a cry of triumph. But Wilma, who, *had* learned a thing or two in all her years of marriage to Ephos, had taken Bran's cue and quietly reversed the barrel – which then unleashed a ray of pure supernatural force upon the prince.

He was momentarily bathed in a sea of light and then, because he had nothing good in his heart, he simply dissolved into nothingness . . . and that was that.

CHAPTER 23

A s you would expect, there was a lot to do after The Wedding That Never Was.

The clear-up was a serious operation. This was organized by Ken aka Dad aka Wisejest, who directed the Bloodswords to dismantle the marquee and redistribute the canapés amongst the grateful citizens.

Effiya was a natural leader and took control of the castle under the principle that she had *almost* been the Queen. There were meetings to be hosted, various delegations from across the Nine Dominions to be seen, treaties to be drawn up, magical creatures to set free. She governed using the lessons from her stories.

One night, the family were sitting on the palace

balcony eating cake and watching Zachary and Zuleka attempt what looked like a rather complicated rhumba in the courtyard. Babadock was there too, and Wilma, and Chidozie, who was enjoying the company of his grandchildren.

Mum sat musing on how her magical absence had effected everyone in the kingdom.

'Was it different before?' Bran asked.

'Yes, Bran,' she answered. 'It was different but not necessarily better. When people rely on magic for everything, they forget to rely on each other. And relying on each other is better for the entire community. Look at what happened when I vanished and the Nine Dominions lost their magic – chaos.'

'Why did you agree to marry Prince Roger in the first place, all those years ago?' Fran asked. 'He's awful.'

Mum sighed. 'I was young. My father had made a match between Prince Roger and me, and I thought this was an opportunity to do good outside of our dominion. We had no idea he was evil – probably because he was so handsome. I only realized once I was living in his palace that he was also the pits. So I ran away and travelled to the earthly domain.

I had no idea that by leaving the Nine Dominions I would upset the balance of magic for everyone around. I'm really very sorry about that.'

Wilma tapped a spoon on her cuppa. 'Now that Prince Roger has gone, I think the Nine Dominions should come together and create a new system for how we are all to live. One without a vain, spoilt prince in charge.'

Mum agreed. She lifted her hands and started signing. At the same time, her voice grew deep and strong – what Fran thought of as her 'storytelling voice'.

'Today marks a new era in Koto Utama and the Nine Dominions. It is up to all of us to work *together* to make us strong and brilliant once more, and rich in *more* than gold, jewels and magic. Bring your best stories and songs and dances and drawings, and make them for everyone. Make them inclusive. Make them smart. Have ambition! And our magical realm will continue to exist for thousands of seasons to come – as we continue to help, respect each other, and absolutely not allow ourselves to be bullied by the bullies, royal or not.'

And her voice, carried by magic, spread to ears and heads across the land.

'We did it,' signed Fran contentedly. She squeezed Bran's hand. 'We saved our parents and we helped the Nine Dominions. It was a true quest.'

Later, Bran went to the throne room and carefully hung up a large illustrated piece of parchment. It contained a cartoon of their adventure – it was colourful and funny and moving, and all that was needed to remind everyone of their adventures, and some hints, in story form of course, of what to do if it happened again. There were copies distributed throughout the Nine Dominions and everyone who read it thought, 'This is fine, but where's the follow-up? What happens next?'

Which is what happens with all the *really good* stories. Right?

For a while, all was peaceful.

But then Mum began to dream again.

Her dreams consisted of stories; tales of rescuers and warriors and talking animals and fantastic food.

But they were also about Ruthvale and Once Upon A Wow and Madge, and how the children loved her stories in the bookshop and how she loved looking at Ken when he was fixing things. She realized she didn't want to be just in the Nine Dominions all the time. She also knew that Bran and Fran needed to go back to school. Fran should have proper singing lessons. Bran wanted to go back to school to prove to himself that he could control his temper and learn how to be a cartoonist.

Effiya sat them all down. After all, in most stories, the main characters always *want* or *need* something. At the beginning, though, they never quite know what those things are . . .

'So,' she said, her shining eyes looking at each of them in turn, 'what is it that you all want?'

They all talked excitedly. 'I miss my Mr Fix-It business,' Ken said wistfully. 'And I think it's time to hand over the role of Chieftain to the next Bloodsword in line. I think Leyna should do us proud – she's great with a broadsword, excellent at signing and she really knows how to deliver a punchline.'

Bran and Fran looked at each other. 'We do *want* to go back to Ruthvale,' Fran said.

'But we'll miss it *here*,' Bran signed. 'And, Mum, you can't go anywhere – you're in charge.'

Mum nodded. 'You're right. The Nine Dominions still need me.'

She thought for a minute.

'What if we could be in the Nine Dominions – *and* at home?'

'How is that possible?' asked Fran, and Mum smiled her beautiful smile.

'Haven't you realized yet? With this family, anything is possible.'

Mum enfolded them all in her arms and told them a story.

The Wizard and his Apprentice

The wizard and his apprentice had been on the longest of journeys.

They had defeated the venomous GODSNAKE. One bite from his jaws and they would have been shrivelled in an instant.

They had taken on SHANGO, the fierce battle spirit. They asked his wife to do them the honour of praying over her husband's grave, and the moment they had done that, the battle spirit disappeared to the happy burial grounds of his colleagues.

They had prevented the evil TREE OF DOOM from spreading its toxic roots throughout the entire Nine Dominions through vigorous use of mystic fire, and they had been almost consumed in their sleep by the nefarious NIGHTMAREGATORS, who snuck into people's dreams and devoured them from within.

So many adventures, so much fun and excitement.

The wizard looked at his apprentice and asked what the girl was looking forward to the most.

The apprentice said, 'I cannot wait to take on our next big adventure. But sometimes I miss my mum's yellow spicy rice and curried mutton and a Nesta soda.'

The wizard replied, 'I look forward to waking up ready to battle. But I also look forward to a hot bath, peppery soup with big pieces of crusty bread, and the love of my family. It is possible to hold two cherished things in your heart at the same time.'

As they were talking, the wizard had transported them home. And as he pointed his apprentice towards her house, where her mum was indeed waiting with yellow spicy rice and curried mutton and a Nesta soda, they both knew that they could call upon each other and embark on a new adventure anytime – but for now, they could enjoy just being at home with family and friends.

The End

CHAPTER

They listened to the story, and when it ended, Mum spoke transformational words of teleportation and with a quiet-ish VA-VA-VA-SHOOOOOOOOOOOOM! they disappeared from one unearthly realm and found themselves back on the other side of the autumnal Kindly Woods near the garage and across from the most dangerous adventure playground in Europe.

Bran signed to Fran, 'That was the most fun I've EVER had in my entire life! It was totally BOSS!'

And Fran looked at him and said, 'I think you'll be fine at school now. Anyone messes with you, and you can just do some of that Bloodsword combat stuff and put them in a hedge.'

Bran laughed and told Fran off for being too fighty.

Ken and Effiya smiled at each other. 'Is it nice to be back, love?' Ken asked. 'It won't be too dull for you?'

And Effiya laughed. 'With you lot? No chance.'

Ken and Effiya set off with their kids, walking up the road to their old house, past Absolutely Kebabulous and the Caribbean Patty Party; past the police station with the broken blue light outside. They walked past Once Upon A Wow and stopped for a moment to see Madge, who was so pleased to see them she almost dropped her fizzy drink. And then they sped the rest of the way home, and Bran and Fran bounded upstairs and put *The Tales of Koto Utama and the Nine Dominions* back in its special place on their shelf. They were home.

But this didn't mean the larger journey was over. They had all their lives to live. They had Auntie Madge to delight and irritate, they had the bookshop to run and they had leaky taps to fix, and singing lessons to attend, and comics to draw.

And, of course, there were endless stories to tell, tales to make them laugh and cry, legends to keep the magic alive.

And whenever they returned to the Nine Dominions they helped Mum as best they could. After all, it was an enormous territory to govern, and there were Zebracorns to see, dragons to ride and magic to learn.

The Nine Dominions would still have problems, and the real world would still have challenges, but thankfully The Dreaming Princess, Wisejest of the Bloodswords, the Boy with the Flying Fingers, and the Girl with the Voice so Pure and Sweet were always on hand to do the right thing.

With a little help from their book of legends.

THE END

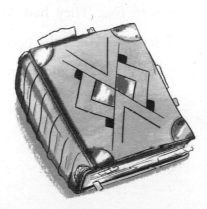

ACKNOWLEDGEMENTS

There's a reason all the famous fantasy novels never have a lone character on a quest – journeys are both easier and more fun with a band of travelling companions. Books, in many ways, are no different. So this is a thank you to my literary travelling companions:

To my editorial team, Samantha Smith, Emily Jones, Genevieve Herr, Nick de Somogyi and Natalie Young. And to Jenna Beacom and Debo Oluwa for their insights.

To the wonderful design and creative team, Keenon Farrell, Fred van Deelen, Rachel Vale and Traccy Ridgewell.

To all the team at Macmillan Children's Books including Alison Ruane, Clare Hall-Craggs, Cheyney Smith, Michele Young, Farzana Khan, Vera Pirri.

To Sarah Clarke, Rachel Graves and all the brilliant sales people across the UK and the world who are making sure this book reaches as many readers as possible.

To my team: Natalie Jerome and Talah, Sanjeev Bhaskar, Neil Reading, Madga Bird and Ellie Humphries.

And of course, as always, a huge thank you to Lisa Milton. There is no one I'd rather journey with.

About the Author

Sir Lenny Henry has risen from being a star on children's television to becoming one of Britain's best-known comedians, as well as a writer, philanthropist and award-winning actor. He is also Co-Founder of the charity Comic Relief. Lenny is a strong advocate for diversity and has recently co-written the book *Access All Areas: The Diversity Manifesto for TV and Beyond*.

About the Illustrator

Keenon Ferrell is an illustrator and animator based in New York. He makes artwork inspired by music, fashion and sports. He also has a love for storytelling, fantasy and history which can be seen throughout his work. Keenon's clients include: Netflix, Capital One, StoryCorps and Sony Music Entertainment, to name a few.

Giammica

Radnuuk

Koto Utama

Deponya

THE MA

NINE DO